Falling for SCOTLAND

KAITLIN COLLINS

Paperback ISBN-13: 979-8-9923956-0-0
Hardback ISBN-13: 979-8-9923956-1-7

Cover design by: Kaitlin Collins
Printed in the United States of America

To all of those who are searching for a gentle love.

Chapter 1

Lydia

I never thought I would be someone who left their long-term job, sold their house, and moved to another country. Yet here I was, unpacking my bags in an apartment in Scotland. I mean, a flat. (I was really going to have to get used to these new terms for things if I didn't want to look like a tourist).

You're probably wondering, 'Now, why, Lydia, would you leave everything to go to Scotland?'. The answer is, I was desperately in need of a change. After working eight years in the American education system, I had lost my passion for a job I'd wanted ever since I was little and the only job I could picture myself doing. Over time, the effect on my mental health had spread to other parts of my life as well. This is my insane attempt to rekindle that love and to just start enjoying life again.

So when I got the email about a program for teachers to work abroad, I clicked the application button without any hesitation. My hope was that the education field might be better somewhere else. Which may just be wishful thinking, but I'm trying to stay positive. Either way, a fresh start was much needed.

Originally, I had hoped for some place sunny and warm like Greece or Spain. I'd already downloaded the Duolingo app in case I needed to learn a new language to survive living on my own in another country. That ended up not being necessary once I received an email with an offer to teach in Scotland. It wasn't exactly known for its sunny and warm weather, but at least I would understand what the locals were saying. Well...mostly.

I warmed up to the idea of Scotland more as I began to research the country. The pictures showed beautiful landscapes ranging from lochs surrounded by mountains to cliffs jutting up out of the ocean. And you can't ignore all the adorable highland cow pictures. It may not be the Mediterranean, but Scotland has its own beauty. Nevermind how interesting the history and folklore is.

A knock on the door made me pause in the midst of placing clothes in the dresser that had finally been delivered. I pushed myself up from the floor with a small groan and made my way to the door, opening it to find the smiling face of another new teacher, Sofia. There were five of us at the school who were here through the teaching abroad program. We had all met at an orientation session last week and were housed in the same building, just down the hall from each other. Sofia was from New Mexico and while that was fairly different from my home state of Missouri, it was nice to not be the only American.

"Did you see Nicolette's text? She said for us all to meet in the lobby."

Oh crap. My eyes darted to the watch on my wrist and then widened. I'd completely lost track of time.

"Just a second! I was unpacking and totally didn't see the text," I called over my shoulder, already hurrying back to the bedroom.

Thank goodness I'd laid my outfit out before I'd started putting things away so I was able to grab it on my way to the bathroom. I dressed hastily and then met my reflection in the mirror, lips pressed together crookedly as I took in my hair. I didn't have curly hair, but it wasn't straight either. My hair had a mind of its own most days with messy waves that did what they wanted. Today was one of those days and I didn't have time to fix it. Ponytail it was. With that handled and just a touch of mascara slapped on, I was presentable enough to go out.

A couple of the veteran teachers were taking us to a Scottish show with traditional music and dancing to introduce us to Scottish cuisine and culture. All I really knew was haggis, which was offered on the menu tonight, and I wasn't too convinced on it. However, I figured the music would be enjoyable and it'd be more time to get to know my coworkers before school started next week and we were busy with lesson plans and students.

"Okay," I breathed out, simultaneously blowing a strand of hair out of my face that had already escaped the confines of my ponytail. "This is as good as it gets."

Sofia just laughed and shook her head at me, an amused grin on her red lips as she watched me throw things into my purse. "You look great, Lydia. A natural beauty."

"You're too kind," I smiled sweetly at her with a small laugh of my own.

She waited for me to lock the door behind us and then we made our way downstairs. The other three were already gathered in the lobby and greeted us before stepping outside to the bus stop. The veteran teachers were meeting us at the show and we were entrusting Nicolette to help us navigate public transportation. Being from France, she was no stranger to buses and metros.

It was mere moments before the bus rumbled up to our stop and we climbed on, managing to find five seats together.

"I hope the men are wearing kilts," one girl smiled conspiratorially. "I want to know if they really do wear nothing underneath."

"Oh mon Dieu!" Nicolette gasped. "And how do you expect to find out?"

She just smirked at all of us and then shrugged

nonchalantly, sending everyone into a fit of giggles. There was more chattering as we bumped along and I was grateful that Nicolette was at least paying attention and knew where we were at.

"Alright, girls. This is us," she announced, already grabbing the back of the seat in front of her, ready to stand.

We all followed suit, standing once the bus had come to a complete stop and filing off. From there it was easy finding the venue; a large sign boasted that the building on our right hosted the "Spirit of Scotland" show. As we neared, our coworkers waved us over and more pleasantries were exchanged while tickets were passed out.

The sound of bagpipes greeted us as soon as we stepped into the lobby, along with girls wearing plaid skirts. Not exactly the men in kilts the others had been hoping for. They checked our tickets and then guided us to our assigned seating. The room was large with three long tables running the length of it; long enough to fit at least twenty people on each side. The stage set gave the illusion that we were seated in the grand hall of a Scottish castle, dim lighting included save the colorful stage lights.

There were plenty of true Scottish castles on my must-visit list. I had gone as far as mapping them out and their distance from Edinburgh so I could plan weekend trips. This mock castle would do for now.

Guests continued to file in as the show time drew

nearer and we took this time to get to know each other better. The veteran teachers were more than willing to answer any questions we had about the school and students. I tried my best to hide my concerns about behaviors, but thankfully Sofia was the one to speak up and ask.

"There seems to be a behavior crisis among students throughout America," she glanced at me when she said this and then back to the Scottish women. "Have you noticed the same problem here?"

Moira pursed her lips, looking at myself and Sofia in a way that I felt suggested pity. "Aye, I've heard of the crisis in America. Shameful it is that ye would have to be put at such risk to your safety while trying to do your job. I don't think it's such a problem here. You'll have the odd wee one that acts foolish now and then, but ye can often put them in their place. And if that doesn't work, ye can be sure their parents will make 'em mind."

"I think that was my biggest problem," I chimed in. "I'd call home about a student and either their parents wouldn't care or they wouldn't know what to do and expected me to tell them how they should handle it."

The others shook their heads in disbelief while Sofia just nodded in agreement. I was once again grateful to have another American who understood where I was coming from and the experiences I'd had. There was more discussion about the teaching situation in America as well as other countries and I found myself extremely grateful when the music grew quiet and the stage lights turned on.

An older gentleman in proper Scottish attire stepped on stage, welcoming us to the show and explaining the order of events for the night. I had to admit that I was quite hungry, having skipped lunch to work on unpacking and trying to get my flat organized before the beginning of the school year. Maybe I'd be so hungry that the haggis would actually taste good!

We were brought drinks along with a starter of either broth or salmon. Not being a fan of fish myself, I had opted for the broth and was grateful for the warmth it brought. I was going to have to get used to this cooler and damp weather. A band played a couple songs as we ate, keeping conversations to a minimum for now which seemed to be fine by all of us. Apparently I wasn't the only one who was hungry.

As the entree was served, our host gave some history of Scotland and the origins of its music and dancing. The two girls who had greeted us came on stage, accompanied by two others and a few men. The men were definitely what had the attention of my colleagues and I noticed Nicolette giggling; most likely remembering the conversation from the bus about the Scottish men and their kilts. Or rather what may or may not be underneath.

I'd be lying, though, if I said the men didn't have my attention as well. Or rather one in particular. He was broader than the others with curly, dark hair and dark stubble to match. He could give *Outlander*'s Sam Hueghan a run for his money, but then again I'd always preferred darker haired men. Despite being a bit bigger than the others, he was light on his feet just the same. Especially when performing the Ghillie Callum, or the Sword Dance, where a pair of swords were laid across one another and the performer nimbly danced over them.

Finishing with a grand bow and a bright smile, the crowd erupted in applause and cheers for the dancers, quite impressed by their performance.

Sofia leaned in once the applause died down, whispering loud enough for everyone in our group to hear, "Never thought I would swoon over a man in a kilt."

"See what I mean?"

"And the dark haired one! Wowza."

There was a small pang of jealousy at another of the women noticing the same man. Not that I had any claim to him and he was obviously attractive. I'm sure women fawned over him at every performance.

The blaring of bagpipes suddenly behind us made us all jump in surprise. The host announced the presentation of the haggis and the men returned with a large platter carried between the four of them. I eyed the dish skeptically. In researching Scottish culture, I had discovered that haggis was prepared in the stomach of a sheep. Just that alone had me wary, not even including what was mixed inside.

However, we all decided to be brave and try it when the haggis was served to us on crackers. Each of us had our phones out, ready to record or snap pictures of our reactions. I hesitantly took a bite, one hand cupped under my mouth to catch any crumbs or fall out. I made sure the bite was big enough that no one would complain and also that I could get a proper idea of how it tasted.

"Not bad," I mumbled around my bite as everyone was anxiously awaiting my verdict. But then I found a chewy lump and couldn't help but scrunch up my nose. "Okay...maybe not that one bit."

The flavor was actually quite good, but I couldn't decide how I felt about the texture. It was an interesting one, that's for sure. Mine was the most tame reaction out of us all, though, with Sofia instantly making a face and shaking her head and Nicolette politely spitting her small bite into her napkin. It seemed as though there was quite the variety of reactions around the hall based on the facial expressions and murmurings of the rest of the audience.

Once the excitement died back down, the host once again stepped on stage. His announcement that audience members would be joining the dancers for a song created almost as much of a reaction out of the crowd as the haggis had. Especially when the dancers began making their way through the tables to select their partners. Or victims depending on how you felt about being on stage, dancing in front of strangers.

Giggling as I watched people encourage their loved ones to go on when a dancer chose them, I was completely unaware of the man making his way towards me. A hand suddenly appeared in front of me and I looked up to meet the chocolate brown eyes of the dancer I'd been admiring all night.

He smiled a charmingly crooked smile down at me and asked, "Fancy a dance?"

I opened my mouth to protest, but my colleagues were all shouting at me to go. Sofia practically shoved me out of my seat and into his arms, leaving me no choice but to take his hand if only to save me from the embarrassment of falling out of my chair. Not that I was sure attempting to perform a Scottish dance would be any less embarrassing.

I knew for a fact that my coworkers would record every single moment. In fact, a glance over my shoulder as I stood showed Moira already pointing her phone at me. She grinned around it and gave me an encouraging thumbs up before her eyes were back on her screen.

All I could do was thank the dim lighting for hopefully hiding how pink my cheeks were as I followed the man towards the stage, his large hand still holding mine. We had just ascended the steps to the stage when a woman appeared from the side and placed her hand on his arm. He paused and bent down for her to whisper in his ear. The crooked smile suddenly disappeared, his face morphing into an expression of serious concern. Without another word, he let go of my hand and disappeared backstage, leaving me standing there alone, unsure what to do.

I was prepared to step back down the stairs, grateful for the excuse no matter how abrupt, when one of the girls caught my hand.

"Come on, lass. I'll dance wi' ye," she smiled encouragingly. "I'm a better dancer anyways."

She sent me a wink and led me further onto the stage. There was little time to wonder about the unexplained disappearance of my original partner as the host began describing the dance steps. In order to not make a fool of myself, this would need all of my attention.

Chapter 2

Alec

I could hear Grandad yelling as soon as I approached the front door; his voice booming throughout the home a stark contrast to the soft, reassuring murmur of his nurse. It only grew louder and more clear as I opened the door and stepped inside.

"I'll no ask ye again! Where is my Ellen? It is past dinner time. She should be here," he demanded, the smallest hint of panic in his voice that made my chest ache.

"Grandad," I called out gently as I stepped into the library. "Don't ye remember?"

His wide eyes turned to me, as well as those of the frazzled nurse. "Oh, Alec, thank goodness," she breathed. Grandad was not as easily soothed.

"What do ye mean, Alec? Where is your grannie?" he insisted.

I calmly walked over to him, despite not feeling the least bit calm after rushing home, and placed my hand reassuringly on his shoulder.

"She went to visit her sister who is ill. That's why Orla

is here," I nodded towards the nurse. "You know Grannie doesna trust us to cook." I sent him a smile that I hoped at least looked somewhat amused.

Either way, he seemed to calm; his shoulder grew less tense under my hand and he resigned to sitting back down. "Aye. Of course." His eyes turned to Orla, "I'm sorry, Ms. Orla, for yelling at ye as I did. I dinna ken where my mind went."

The nurse waved it away dismissively. This wasn't his first fit that she'd experienced, whether he knew that or not. "You're alright, Mr. Morgan. I know ye love your Ellen and just want to make sure she's safe."

Grandad nodded silently, his gaze already elsewhere and most likely his mind, too. Orla bent to pick up the cup he had apparently knocked off the side table and then made her way to the kitchen. I followed close behind.

"I'm sorry I called ye, Alec. I ken ye were working tonight, but he willna listen to anyone but you when he's in that state."

I nodded knowingly. "It's alright, Orla. I'm glad ye called when ye did. We both know it could've been much worse."

Grandad had received a diagnosis of Alzheimer's disease just over a year ago. At first it was fine enough that a nurse could check in on him daily and family periodically. But the disease had progressed enough that it was no longer possible for him to live alone. So we hired Orla full time and I moved to Edinburgh to look after Grandad. My parents had yet to retire and neither could leave their job to care for him full time. Then there was my brother, Archie, who lived close enough in Glasgow, but he had a wife and three children to look after. So the responsibility fell to me; the son with no family of his own yet who worked remote and therefore could work anywhere. Perks of being an editor, I suppose.

I was glad to do it, though. Growing up, I had been Grandad's best friend and he'd been mine. In fact, he was the one who fostered my love of literature, being an English professor until he absolutely had to retire. There was nothing better than spending a rainy evening in his library with a fire going; him reading a novel he'd probably read a thousand times judging by the worn cover and myself editing the newest manuscript my company had sent me. All in all, I was grateful for the opportunity and did not see it as a burden I had to take on. If anything, it was a gift getting to spend what time I could with him. While he was still himself, that is.

As for the dancing in the "Spirit of Scotland" show, I had simply picked that up as a means of extra cash. And of course, there were times I needed to get out of the house and spend time around people who weren't my Grandad. Forget about the sad parts of life for a bit. The other performers and crew members of the show definitely helped with that.

I groaned and bent over to rest my elbows on the counter, burying my hands in my hair as I remembered the girl from the show tonight. Not a girl. Definitely a woman and a beautiful one at that. And I had completely left her standing there alone on the stage after plucking her from the audience despite her protests. She must've been mortified. I'd have to ask the others what happened after I left and could only hope that one of them had rescued her from complete embarrassment.

Orla eyed me suspiciously as she stirred something in a pot on the stove. "What's that all about? Did something else happen tonight?"

I shook my head at first, now placing my palms to the counter and standing upright. "While I dinna mind ye calling me, I do wish ye had better timing," I allowed. "I had just chosen a partner from the audience for the final dance when Elize grabbed me. I didna think and just left the girl standing there without any explanation."

I should've explained to her or at the least, told her that there was an emergency and I was terribly sorry. Instead, I had dashed off without a thought about anything else besides Grandad.

My skin began to itch under the watchful gaze of Orla. She had a way of looking at you and making you feel as if she could read your mind. I believe it's why Grandad liked her so much. She would already be up getting whatever it was he needed before he'd even opened his mouth to ask.

"What?" I finally asked.

Orla smiled knowingly as she adjusted the burner's temperature. "She was a bonnie lass, wasn't she?"

I rolled my eyes, but that just made her grin even wider knowing that she had been correct. Mind reader, I tell ye. "Aye, she was," I admitted. "But she was American. I'm sure she'll be out of Edinburgh by morning and it's not like I'd ever see her again anyways."

Thankfully, the opportunity to run into an audience member after the show was rare and anybody I did know in Edinburgh wasn't going to go to a show displaying their own culture and heritage. For the most part, I was safe from anyone recognizing me or knowing that I danced in a kilt for extra cash. It didn't exactly fit with my usual introverted personality.

"Ye never know," Orla shrugged. "What's for ye'll no go by ye."

What's meant to be, will be. "Maybe it's time we have your mind checked out as well, Ms. Orla."

"Och!" she scoffed and waved her dishtowel at me. That was clearly my sign to get out of the kitchen and make better use of myself. Like getting out of this kilt for one.

Grandad had woken up in a much better mood and with a craving specifically for tattie scones. We were somehow out of potatoes, so it was off to the market I went. It wasn't like I had plans for the day anyways and the sky had decided not to rain for the first day all week. Grandad really couldn't have had better timing. I left him in the house watching *Fawlty Towers* reruns and made my way to the market a few blocks over. Orla had the day off, but I was sure Grandad would be fine on his own long enough for me to do some shopping.

Everyone seemed to have the same idea to make use of the sunshine and were out and about. Normally I may grumble and complain about having to deal with other people while trying to run errands, but my mood was considerably chipper today. Surely I couldn't fault them for also enjoying the break from the rain.

As I walked past a pub, I spotted a somewhat familiar head of light auburn hair; the woman from last night's show. A pang of guilt hit me as I remembered her confusion when I'd left her on the stage alone. I owed her an apology and at least somewhat of an explanation. Orla's reminder also made its way back to the forefront of my mind. What's meant for ye'll no go by ye. It appeared so.

Her hair was blowing about her face while she gazed into the window of a book shop, eyes skimming over the covers of the displayed novels, completely undisturbed by the obstruction her hair created. She looked up at the sudden appearance of another reflection in the glass and I could see the surprise on her face fade into slight recognition. A small crease appeared between her eyebrows as she turned to take me in, but the curve of her lips suggested that she wasn't upset. Hopefully.

"You're the guy from the Scotland show, aren't you? My runaway dance partner," she guessed.

I rubbed the back of my neck, head ducked slightly as I gave her a sheepish smile that was somewhat closer to a grimace. "Yeah. I uh...I'm really sorry about leaving ye like that. Hopefully I didn't embarrass ye too terribly?"

She shrugged with a small roll of her eyes upward in a 'what can you do' way. "My coworkers did heckle me some when I got back to my seat after dancing with one of the girls. They asked if I smelled bad or had done something else to scare you off."

That made me chuckle, but I was quick to shake my head, holding my hands out toward her in reassurance. "No, no. I assure ye, ye didna smell bad. It's just, Elize told me I had a call from the nurse about my Grandad and she never calls when I'm doing a show. So I knew it was urgent."

"Oh. Is he okay?" she asked, all joking gone from her face and instantly replaced with genuine concern. I fought the urge to smile at that. Her green eyes looked really pretty, all big and innocent.

"Aye. Well I mean...no, but-" I frowned and there was that quirk of a smile in the corner of her lips again. "It's a bit of a long story and I'm sure ye've got better things to do."

She just shrugged once more, "Honestly, I'm just exploring. Enjoying my last day before school starts."

"Oh. Headed back to the states then?" I won't lie and say I wasn't disappointed to find this out. Something about her just made me feel at ease and there were few people like that in my life.

Now it was her turn to avert her gaze, her hand reaching up to tuck a stray hair behind her ear. "Actually, I'm teaching here this year."

My eyebrows furrowed, "You came all the way here to teach?" It seemed a little silly to me to come to such a gloomy place just to spend your days with snotty-nosed children. But to each their own I supposed. Not like I had room to judge, putting on a kilt and dancing in front of tourists.

"It's a..." she laughed a little self-deprecatingly, "...bit of a long story."

"Ah," I nodded. This time when I smiled at her, she returned it and that feeling of ease washed over me once more. "Well, if you're out and about exploring, you'll definitely need to visit the Thistle. Wonderful cafe just down the way." I inclined my head down the street in the original direction I'd been heading.

She followed my gaze over her shoulder and then turned her smile to me once more. Quite the charming smile it was. "Would you mind showing me?"

I hesitated only because of Grandad. He was expecting me to be back soon and to fix his tattie scones. But honestly, would he even realize that I was gone longer than usual? He tended to lose track of time when he was watching *Fawlty Towers* and not to mention how much of a scolding I would get from Orla if she found out that I had run into the girl from the show again and then let her slip away once more.

"Not at all," I responded without another thought. "Follow me."

I tipped my head in the direction of the cafe and waited for her to start walking before falling in step beside her. We were quiet as we walked and she continued to glance in the windows of each place we passed. My eyes were clearly on her, so I saw the light pink at the apple of her cheeks when she turned her face to me and met my gaze.

"I'm Lydia, by the way," she blurted suddenly, holding

her hand out to me.

I just chuckled and took her hand in my own, giving it a firm but gentle shake. "Alec," I nodded.

We fell back into silence, but I wouldn't exactly call it a comfortable silence. Obviously we had our stories to tell, if she wanted to hear it that is, but walking down the street wasn't exactly the place I'd like to give the spiel of why I lived with my Grandad. Thankfully, the cafe was only a couple shops down the street from the bookstore. I hesitated outside the door. While she had asked me to show her the way, she hadn't explicitly said whether she'd like for me to join her or not.

As if she read my mind, she turned to me with that bright smile of hers. "Would you like to join me? Maybe share that long story of yours over a cup of tea?" her brows rose hopefully.

I couldn't help but smile back. "I'd love to."

Grandad would just have to wait on his tattie scones. Surely, he would understand once I explained the situation.

I followed her inside and we joined the queue in front of the pastry display. Maybe I could make it up to Grandad by bringing him back a tart; he was a sucker for desserts. Mind made up about that, I looked over their menu for tea options, Lydia doing the same. She then leaned towards me and her hair brushed my arm.

"I'll be honest. I'm more of a sweet iced tea person," she whispered conspiratorially. "What would you recommend?"

Oh, Americans and their concept of tea, I mentally shook my head. "Personally, I am more of an Earl Grey guy. Very simple. But if ye like sweeter teas, I would recommend chamomile."

"Chamomile it is," she decided with a definitive nod. "Maybe I'll branch out more in the future." She sent me a smirk then and again, I couldn't help but smile back.

When it was our turn to order, I took the initiative to not only order for the both of us, but to pay as well.

"Oh, you don't have to do that," Lydia fussed a little, but I simply waved her off.

"Please. It's the least I can do for ye after leaving ye stranded."

"Fair."

She grinned and I grinned back until the barista was returning my credit card to me. I tucked it into my wallet with a quick thank you and then turned to find a spot for us to sit. I didn't even think as I placed my hand at the small of Lydia's back to gently nudge her towards a table near the windows to wait for our drinks, but I was quick to remove it as soon as she started in that direction. The last thing I needed to do was embarrass myself by making her uncomfortable.

Chapter 3

Lydia

I prayed that Alec didn't feel me stiffen at the touch of his hand, but it had taken me by surprise. Which I scolded myself for since he had held my hand just last night. But of course, that was to guide me through a dark room to the stage and he held someone's hand every night he performed. I was nothing special.

Trying not to overthink it, I instead focused on making my way to the empty table and hanging my purse along the back of the chair before taking a seat. Alec settled into the chair across from me and I once again noted how captivating his eyes were. Now seeing them in the sunlight instead of a dark room, I could see just how much of a warm, chocolate color they had. I really needed to stop staring or he was going to think I was a total creep.

"So..." I started, propping my elbows on the table and folding my hands together for my chin to rest on. "Do we share our long stories now or wait for the tea?"

His dark brows rose. "Wow. Just really getting to it, huh?"

I shrugged, "Might as well. No need for small talk."

"I see. Well I suppose I should go first since I'm the one who owes ye an explanation for last night." I waited patiently as he visibly organized his thoughts, drawing a line with his finger along the tabletop. "My Grandad has Alzheimer's. We're in the early stages, but it's getting progressively worse. He's started to have bouts of anger and typically his nurse canna calm him down. Suppose he doesna fully recognize her in those moments, so I'm pretty much the only one who can get him settled. He had a bad fit last night and Orla called for my help."

I nodded understandingly, but my brain was trying to process what that must be like for him. I'd never had personal experience with Alzheimer's, but I knew it was a nasty disease that slowly stripped away a person you loved until you didn't recognize them anymore. And they didn't recognize you. I couldn't imagine being in Alec's place; knowing how it all would end.

"You must be very close to your Grandad if he finds your presence so reassuring," I mused softly. That at least brought a small smile to the corner of his lips.

"Aye. We're best friends. He used to say I was the miniature version of him," he tilted his head as one shoulder came up in a shrug. "Obviously, I'm no so miniature now, but ye get the picture. He was an English professor and I would spend summers absolutely devouring the books in his library. Nights would be spent discussing what I read with him and our thoughts on it."

I tried to picture a small, curly-haired boy sitting in a library with books spread all about him while his grandfather looked on. It was quite an adorable image. His expression however had grown somber once more and he gave one small nod, just a tip of his chin.

"He needs more care now as the disease has progressed, so I moved here to live with him and look after him."

"That's very admirable of you, Alec. Not that you need my validation, of course, but..." I let it trail off, not exactly sure what to say.

"Och, look who's talking. You're the one teaching children and that's no an easy job, I'm sure."

My cheeks puffed up and I let out a breath, having to resist from rolling my eyes and instead glancing out the window. "Oh you have no idea," I mumbled under my breath.

Just then, the barista approached with our teas, setting them down in front of us along with a small box for Alec. I recalled him asking for a tart, but he didn't open it, instead nudging it to the side and then moving his tea in front of him so he could gently blow on it. His warm eyes then flicked up to me across the rim as he took a sip.

"Seems now is the time for your long story."

I sighed once more as I cradled my cup in my hands. "I suppose so."

Now it was my turn to organize my thoughts and figure out what exactly to share. People abroad had their own opinions of America and I didn't want to exactly reaffirm any of the negative ones, but it was hard not to when I thought of my past experiences in the classroom. Besides, he had been very open and honest with me about his grandfather. Surely, I could do the same.

"I've taught for eight years, but I stopped really enjoying it a couple years ago now." It was always difficult to describe to people outside of the education field. While most everyone had attended school at some point in their lives, they hadn't been an educator and that was a totally different ball park. "I began having panic attacks in the morning before work, worried about what the day would entail and what exactly I would have to deal with. Add on the lack of support from parents and administration and it was just a recipe for disaster."

I took a careful sip of my tea and even though I was looking out the window once more, I could feel Alec's eyes on me as he listened intently.

"But I don't know what else I would do. I've wanted to be a teacher ever since I was little and it used to bring me so much joy. So...I thought a change of scenery might help. Maybe bring back a spark or something. I don't know." I shook my head with a disappointed sigh, unsure if I was being naive in that hope.

Alec's head tilted to the side, making it so that I had to look at him now. His expression was gentle and there was an echo of understanding in his eyes.

"You've still got the passion for it. I can tell just in the way ye talk about teaching," he encouraged, his voice soft. He cocked his head to the side then. "Now, I dinna ken if these wee heathens here are any better than the ones at home for ye. I'm no so good with them myself, but I ken that the families will support you. Teachers are highly regarded here."

Just that last sentiment made me feel more at ease and confident in my decision. Add on that Moira had said something along the same lines yesterday.

"Thank you," I spoke just as gently as he had.

We quietly sipped our tea in silence for a little bit. My gaze once more wandered out the window to the bustling street. Seems I wasn't the only one who had decided today was a good day to be out and about. The sun reflecting through the glass was warm on my skin and I knew I needed to enjoy it while I could.

"If anything, I get the chance to explore Scotland," I shrugged with a smile.

"Have ye ever been before?"

I shook my head. "No, but I did some research before I

came and have already started a list of places to visit on my breaks or on the weekend."

"Oh really?" Alec eyed me curiously, a dark brow cocked. "Let me see this list then. See if ye have anything of real quality."

I dropped my jaw slightly with a light scoff, but dug my phone out of my purse anyway to open the notes app. Then I slid it across the table to him and watched intently as he picked it up to read over what I'd written down. Every now and then he'd make a small noise that I couldn't quite decipher the meaning of. Was it approval or disappointment? Then he suddenly looked up at me, thumb hesitating over the screen.

"Mind if I add a few?"

I shook my head. "Not at all. I'd much rather take advice from a native Scot than from some travel blog," I amended. That at least erased the wrinkle between his brows and brought a smile back to the corner of his lips.

"Smart lass."

He looked back at my phone and began to add to the list, thumbs moving swiftly over the screen. I drank the last of my tea and sat back as I waited for him to finish.

"There," he finally slid my phone back and then reached for his own cup. "Added my number as well."

I looked down at my phone in shock, but there it was; his new contact page pulled up with the information filled out just like he'd stated. Alec Morgan.

"Surprised you didn't add a picture while you were at it," I managed to tease.

He just laughed and finished off his drink before taking both of our empty cups to toss in the bin behind him. Just then, my phone buzzed in my hand and the little message preview box appeared on the screen, showing a text from Sofia. Alec must've noticed the alert as well.

"I'm sure you've got other places to be and things to do before work starts tomorrow." I opened my mouth to disagree, but he just smiled and held up a hand to stop me. "It's alright. I was actually on my way to the market and Grandad will be wondering where I'm at soon enough."

He stood, but waited for me to stand as well before walking towards the door with me. We both hesitated on the sidewalk, not really sure of ourselves.

"Well, tell your Grandad I said hi," I smiled with a shrug before making a face and shaking my head. "I'm sorry. That was really weird. He has no clue who I am. Hell, you barely know who I am."

Alec just smiled patiently, his brows raised in amusement as he waited for me to finish rambling.

"Have a good day, Alec," I summed up lamely.

"Have a good day, Lydia, and best of luck tomorrow," he nodded his head. "If ye ever want a free tour guide, you've got my number now."

"Right. Thank you."

To save myself any further embarrassment, I turned and started walking. Not that I knew where I was going, but it was the opposite direction of Alec and that was all I needed to know as I felt my cheeks burn crimson. Still, I couldn't hide the smile on my face either.

Chapter 4

Alec

"Did ye get lost or something, laddie?" Grandad asked as I stepped through the sitting area to the kitchen, his furry eyebrows tightly knit together. He followed behind me, eyeing the bags I carried. "The market isna very far."

"Aye, I know, Grandad. I just got a bit distracted, but I got ye a berry tart to make up for it."

His eyes lit up at that and he eagerly took the small box from me, opening it up and peering inside. Then his grin was turned to me and he reached out to ruffle my hair, making the dark curls stick up in odd places.

"You're a good lad."

He removed the tart from the box and took a bite, happily humming around it. Clearly he wasn't going to wait for his tattie scones. They were long forgotten in favor of the sweet pastry.

"Tart for breakfast, then?" I eyed him with a grin as I put away the rest of the purchases. I still kept the potatoes out anyways, knowing that the tart wouldn't fill him up.

"Och. I'm eighty-four years old. I can have dessert

whenever I want," he grumbled, a couple crumbs falling onto his white beard.

I just laughed and nodded my head in assent, "I canna argue that."

Pleased, he made his way over to the small table in the window alcove and sat to enjoy the rest of his treat. I made sure to pour him a cup of tea before I started cooking. He merely hummed in thanks as I placed the saucer down in front of him and then went back to the treat.

The tourist season was dying down as the summer began to come to a close and I wasn't sure if I preferred it or not. While it did mean I had less shows to perform in, it also meant the crowds were smaller and that made it more awkward when picking a partner. Granted, that was already an extremely awkward situation. Maybe if I was an extrovert, I would thrive off the thrill of picking a stranger to pull onto stage and dance with. But alas, I was fairly introverted and felt a twinge of panic each time.

Most of the people chosen did not have a musical bone in their body, no matter how hard I tried to scope out someone who was at least clapping to the beat of the other songs. Overall, it was a fairly simple dance in my opinion, but some people had two left feet as they say.

Tonight's partner had been especially painful; an older woman who continued to step on my toes, only to apologize by placing her hand on my chest. Over and over. Or at least that's what I assumed she was saying, as she didn't speak a lick of English. Either way, I was all too eager to guide her back to her table after the dance and away from my throbbing toes.

At least the show was almost over and I just had one more short dance to do for the finale before we sent the tourists on their way and I was able to go home. And apparently ice my feet.

I was stripping off my costume before I'd even fully made it into the dressing room and tossing it into the dirty hamper costuming left for us by the door, the other male performers hot on my heels.

"Oi. Looks like Alec has a secret admirer," Graham called out.

I rolled my eyes as I tugged my shirt over my head, making sure to meet his gaze in the mirror while I ran my fingers through my curls in an attempt to tame them.

"She was practically feeling ye up out there."

Subconsciously, I ran my hand over my chest. "Aye. Not a shy one, was she?"

We all had a good laugh at that. There was nothing we

could do but laugh at the antics of our guests. People had no shame when they were on vacation. Especially when they could plead that they didn't understand what you were saying.

Once I had redressed and put all my things away, I bid the others goodbye and headed out the back entrance to my car. After tonight, I was more than ready to sink into one of the overstuffed leather chairs in the library and relax. Maybe edit some of the current novel I was working on.

My phone buzzed as soon as I started the engine and I paused to get it out of my pocket, a small flicker of worry shooting through me that it might be about Grandad. The tight feeling in my chest didn't go away when my phone buzzed a second time and I saw who exactly it was.

Unknown Number

What does bampot mean?

This is Lydia btw

I couldn't help but chuckle, swiping the message open so that I could type out a reply.

It means 'idiot'. Why? Did one of the wee brats call you one?

I found myself waiting for her response instead of driving away, watching those three bubbles bounce up and down as she typed. When I'd put my number in her phone, I had stupidly forgotten to ask for her number in return or send myself a text from her phone. I was at least proud of myself for being brave enough to add myself to her contacts in the first place. *Well done on that, Alec.*

I'd feared that she'd found me too forward and would delete it as soon as possible. So I was more than pleased that I had been wrong and she had reached out.

Lydia

> No, thank goodness. (Though they wouldn't be the first)

> I was having the students describe their family and one boy described his brother as a bampot.

> Aye, I see. Sounds like a typical brother.

Suddenly there was a tap on my window and I practically jumped out of my skin, dropping my phone into my lap as I looked up to find Elize peering in at me.

"Are ye alright?" she asked, voice muffled through the glass.

I hastily rolled the window down so she could hear me better. "Aye. Sorry. Was just responding to a text," I explained sheepishly.

Elize nodded. "Good. Just wanted to make sure there was nothing wrong with your Grandad. I know his fits can come back to back at times."

That was one of the things I appreciated most about my coworkers at the show is how much they cared for each other. I wasn't the only one going through tough times, but we always made sure that we were there to support one another. It was like having a little family.

"Thank ye for checking on me, Elize. I do appreciate it."

She just nodded and smiled before standing upright and sending a wave over her shoulder as she made her way back to her car. Figuring I should stop sitting there smiling at my phone like a bampot, I finally put my car in reverse and pulled out of the parking lot to head home.

Grandad was sat in the study reading next to the hearth, his glasses precariously perched on the end of his nose. He looked very much the professor that he was. Or had been. Even if he had retired years ago, he never stopped researching and imparting what knowledge he had collected over the years onto myself and Orla. Whether Orla cared to know or not.

He looked up when I entered and closed the tome he was reading before reaching up to take off his glasses.

"How was tonight's show?" he asked, genuinely curious. I just sighed a deep heavy sigh as I sank into the chair across from him. "Like that, then, eh?"

"Let's just say, I'm nervous to take off my shoe and find my big toe to be purple."

He grimaced at that, but still chuckled as he folded up his glasses and set them to the side. "Not everyone can be as light on their feet as you, Alec," he winked at me.

A love of literature wasn't the only thing Grandad had passed down to me. It was he who taught me and Archie the traditional Scottish dances. Grandad was a Scot through and through and very proud of it. I sometimes joked with him that he should've been a history major as well, but he always argued that the history books got it wrong and he much preferred the recallings of true authors.

My phone buzzing in my pocket once more brought me out of my reverie and I eagerly pulled it out of my pocket, only to frown when I saw my brother's name.

"Hoping it'd be someone else?" Grandad asked knowingly, though his voice portrayed nonchalance as he stood to put away the book. I was itching to tell someone about Lydia and there was no one better than Grandad.

"Actually, yes."

"And is this person the reason ye took so long at the market?"

He may be losing his memory, but nothing got past Grandad. Especially when it came to me. He knew me better than anyone.

"Yes," I nodded, a hint of warmth in my cheeks that I tried to blame on the small fire. "Her name is Lydia. She was at the show last week and I pulled her up to dance, but I-" I coughed to clear my throat, not wanting to tell him I'd had to leave her to come home to him. He didn't usually remember his fits and I liked to keep it that way. No need to make him feel burdened. "I didna get her number, of course. Dinna think it'd be appreciated. But then I ran into her on the way to the market and took her to the Thistle for a cup of tea."

Grandad was smiling. He returned to his seat and looked at me with the same interest he did his books. "Tell me about her, then, if she's got ye smiling like that."

I hadn't even noticed I was. I tried to wipe it off my face, but it was hard when I thought back on Lydia standing there with the sun glinting off her copper hair, completely unaware of the bustle around her.

"Well, she's American, but she's here for a year to teach at a local school."

"Bonnie?"

"Aye. Long, light auburn hair and these green eyes that ye canna help but fall into." They reminded me of Scotland hills in the spring, the bright green amongst the heather giving you hope that there were warmer days ahead.

Grandad wore a similar expression to what I assumed I wore, though his eyes were distant as he gazed into the fire. "Your grannie had eyes like that. Dark as the loch and I felt as though I would drown in them, but happily so."

Grannie and Grandad had the kind of love the poets wrote about and I was blessed to have witnessed such an all encompassing love as I grew up. It was a love that transcended time and even diseases of the mind. I was sure that Grandad would never forget her, no matter how much he lost.

"I remember they used to sparkle."

Grandad chuckled and nodded, "Aye. She was quite magical," he agreed. He was quiet for a few moments more and I wasn't sure where he had gone, but I wasn't about to pull him out of it. I could tell it was a good place, full of happy memories. Soon enough his gaze cleared and was more focused as he turned his own sapphire eyes to me. "Are ye going to see this Lydia again?"

"Well I'd like to," I admitted, nervously rubbing the back of my neck.

Between moving to Edinburgh and looking after Grandad, my love life hadn't exactly been at the forefront of my thoughts and concerns, but I couldn't stop thinking about Lydia. Which was ridiculous given that I'd only seen her twice and had one decent conversation. Still.

"Then tell her. What's stopping ye?" Grandad asked incredulously.

He was right. As always.

"I will, I will," I assured him.

That seemed to please him and we fell back into amicable silence as the fire began to fade to embers.

Chapter 5

Lydia

Sofia and I were enjoying our lunch break in her room today. She'd left the lights off save a few lamps and we'd shut the door in hopes of not being interrupted. It was a nice pocket of peace before the kids would return. Not that I could complain; The year had started off great and it just made me more hopeful that I had in fact made the right choice.

I had yet to tell her about running into Alec and I felt a little guilty about keeping it to myself. In just a couple weeks, Sofia had easily become my best friend here. We often spent evenings working on lesson plans together in one of our flats before ending the night with a glass of wine and some TV show we both enjoyed. Every so often, Nicolette would join us for dinner. It was nice spending time with them, especially being so far from home. Living in a different time zone made regular conversations with family and friends difficult, so I was more than grateful for my little family I was building here.

"Do you, um, remember the guy from the Scotland

show?" I blurted during a small lapse in conversation, poking at my lunch with my fork.

"You mean tall, dark, and handsome? How could I forget him?" she asked, earning a chuckle from me. "I still can't believe that he just left you without an explanation after picking you out of the audience. As if being pulled on stage isn't embarrassing enough!"

I opened my mouth and then shut it again, trying to work out how exactly to say this. I'd been dying to talk to someone about Alec, though. Maybe talking about him would confirm that he was in fact real and I hadn't just dreamed him up. I mean, running into him had been something straight out of a romantic movie. Far too good to be true, but his contact in my phone proved to me that it was real.

"So um...I ran into him the next day and he gave me his number."

Sofia's jaw dropped practically to the floor, her fork paused midway to her mouth. "Shut up. And you're just now telling me this?!"

I held my hands up to ward her off, should she be inclined to use that fork for stabbing other things besides her pasta. Thankfully she set it down, turning her body so it was facing me completely, dark eyes locked on me.

"Tell me everything."

I caught her up on how I'd ran into Alec while

exploring on Sunday and that we'd gotten tea together. I also told her about his reasoning for disappearing at the show, but didn't share too much in case he liked to keep that more private; simply stating that he'd had a family emergency and was very apologetic. She practically keeled over when I told her he'd confidently put his number in my phone.

"Are you going to see him again? Please, tell me you are."

I shrugged my shoulders helplessly, "I don't know. I've only texted him one time since then and he hasn't reached out since."

Sure, he was probably busy with work and his grandfather, but I wasn't about to come off as some needy girl. That wasn't my style.

"Text him and ask him to come to the pub with us and Nicolette this weekend."

I gave her a small look. "Do you really think he wants to come out with a bunch of foreign girls?"

"Um, yeah! Especially if one of them is you!"

I just shook my head at her and returned to my food, but I couldn't deny that the idea was appealing. At this point, I'd take any excuse to see him.

"I'll think about it."

Sofia just gave me a knowing look as she picked back up her fork and began eating again. I was grateful when the conversation moved onto something else she'd thought of and the attention was off of me.

I paced the living room of my flat, dodging boxes, my phone tapping anxiously against my leg as I tried to work up the courage to text Alec. Normally I was not big on texting, finding that the meaning of messages could be too easily misconstrued, but I didn't know if he was working or not. Then again, I could always leave a voice message.

In a sudden burst of blind confidence, I finally pressed the phone icon to call him, continuing to pace as the line rang. It seemed to go on forever and I was sure that I would end up with his voicemail when there was sudden silence and then a deep "Hullo?"

"Hi. Alec? It's Lydia," I explained quickly, nerves evident in my voice despite my best efforts to stay calm. Who was I kidding?

He chuckled softly and I relaxed a little at the sound of it. "I ken it's you, Lydia. I added ye to my contacts after ye texted me last."

"Right. Of course." He waited patiently as I organized my thoughts; I hadn't exactly been prepared for him to answer. "So I was just calling to see if you'd like to join some of my friends and me at a pub this weekend? Two of the girls that were with me at the show. Figured you'd know the best place to go."

"Oh, so you're just using my services as a local to find a good place, then?" he teased.

"No. I just...I'm going out with friends, so I figured I'd invite you since you're my friend as well." I squeezed my eyes shut and was grateful he wasn't standing there in front of me. *God, Lydia, how much of a dork could you be? Your friend?* "Or, well, you're one of the few people I know here, I mean."

"Lydia," he interrupted gently. "I'd love to. I can text ye the address for a good spot and meet ye there. Just let me know when."

"Do you have a show this weekend?"

"No. I've taken the weekend off since I've got a due date coming up for the book I'm editing. Besides...the shows are starting to slow down with the tourist season coming to a close."

I'd finally stopped pacing and sat down on my couch, but still nibbled on the fingernail of my thumb, a terrible habit. "Okay. Then how about Saturday?"

"Saturday it is. I'll send ye the address soon."

"Great! Thanks."

There was a long moment of silence, neither of us

hanging up, but we weren't saying anything either. I had just opened my mouth to say goodbye, figuring that was the end of the conversation when I was interrupted by Alec's question.

"Are ye busy planning your lessons?" he wondered.

"Oh. No. I'm all planned out for this week. I'm just trying to get my flat set up. I've had some more things come in that I ordered."

"I wondered what that process would look like, what with moving halfway across the world."

I laughed a little as I glanced around at the small flat. It was rather chaotic at the moment with boxes scattered throughout, half of them opened and half still full of things. Some of it I had my family ship to me from Missouri and other things I had purchased to be delivered. What I would do with it all after my year teaching here was another matter that future Lydia could worry about.

My goal was to make the flat as homey as possible and to also bring in some color to combat the typical gloomy skies of Scotland. So far I had set up most of the furniture and a few pieces of decor; mostly plants I'd purchased or pictures I'd brought from home of family and friends. It still had a ways to go for my liking, but I was getting there.

"Well, I still have things that haven't arrived yet, so it'll be a work in progress for a while," I amended. "But it gives me something to do after work."

"Aye. I'm sure ye'll have it all to your liking soon enough." I smiled at his encouragement, finding comfort in the support even if it was from somewhat of a stranger. "I'll leave ye to it, then, and plan on seeing you girls on Saturday."

I nodded even though he couldn't see me. "See you Saturday. Goodbye, Alec."

"Goodbye, Lydia."

Pressing the red button to end the call, I was glad to not have anyone around to see the giddy smile on my face. Sofia and Nicolette wouldn't have let me hear the end of it. Saturday was definitely going to be interesting with them.

Not wanting to worry about that now, I returned to the box closest to me and removed the knitted, yellow blanket. Cozy blankets were always essential in a home, but I'd be especially grateful for it on rainy days and when the temperatures started to drop in the coming months. Add on that it perfectly matched the yellow throw pillows I had ordered as well.

I laid it across the arm of the couch for now and stepped back to take in the living room. It was finished for the most part. Over the next few weeks, I hoped to collect some more decor items, but I had the necessities. While it was only one part of the flat, I still felt accomplished at having gotten everything in its place. Now my friends and I could spend time in my flat without it feeling so bare.

I pushed the thought away of spending an evening in this space with Alec. That was thinking way too far ahead and it would honestly be a miracle if Nicolette didn't scare him off this weekend. She was quite the extrovert with no filter and no shame in telling the truth. But I loved her for it all the same.

Yes, Saturday would be interesting indeed.

Chapter 6

Lydia

"Lyds! Where is your curling iron?" Nicolette called from the small bathroom attached to my room.

As much time as I had spent organizing my bedroom and bathroom over the last couple of days, my friends had created a significant mess in the two spaces as we all got ready to go out. Our makeup bags looked as if they had exploded on the bathroom counter and here on the floor in front of my full-length mirror where I was currently sitting cross-legged attempting to do my eyeshadow while Sofia stood over me applying lipstick in the reflection.

Nicolette, extremely indecisive on what to wear, had brought over an armful of clothes for us to give her an opinion on. The rejected items were now tossed on the end of my bed.

"Basket on the shelf above the toilet. One closest to the sink," I instructed, pausing in my application to make sure she found it.

There was a bit of rustling noise from the bathroom before I heard a triumphant, "Found it! Merci!"

"De rein," I replied.

Nicolette laughed as she popped her head out of the bathroom, the warming curling iron in her hand.

"Lydia. It is not 'day ree-on'. You say 'duh ree-on'," she explained, using her hand to emphasize the 'duh'.

I did my best to mimic her, feeling quite silly, but she graced me with a smile and a nod. "Better." Then she disappeared back into the bathroom to do her hair.

Sofia laughed softly above me as she finished up, placing the cap back on her tube of lipstick. Then she began to gather all of her products that were scattered about. I wasn't far behind, just adding some mascara to my light brown eyelashes so I actually had lashes and then beginning to clean up as well. It would all be much more manageable when it was only Nicolette's things left.

"Nic, do you want us to take your rejected clothing back to your place?" Sofia asked, leaning against the doorframe to the bathroom.

"Oh, that would be lovely. Merci, mon cher."

"I have no idea what you just called me, but no problem."

With that, she made her way over to the bed and tried to somewhat organize the pile.

"Here, let me help you." I took half of the pile, trying not to let anything fall as we made our way to the front door and down the hall to Nicolette's flat. We each had a spare key to each other's flats now and thankfully Sofia had her keys currently on her.

Where my flat was full of yellows and greens, Nicolette's was full of dusty pinks. It seemed very French to me, but maybe that was just my bias of growing up with friends having rooms that were hot pink and black and covered in Eiffel Towers. Either way, her decor was elegant and spot on for Nicolette.

Sofia and I took it upon ourselves to hang up her clothing instead of leaving it to wrinkle on her bed. By the time we were back at my place, she had finished curling her hair. It was short and a caramel brown, the curls making it frame her petite face perfectly.

"You look beautiful, Nic," I gushed.

"And look at the two of you. Alec isn't going to know what to do in the presence of such devastatingly gorgeous women."

"Don't worry. His eyes will be on Lydia the whole night," Sofia insisted, nudging me playfully.

My cheeks instantly burned, "Oh, whatever." I couldn't help but hope she was right, though, because I knew my eyes would be on him.

Once my flat had been restored for the most part and we had our purses, we made our way downstairs to find a cab. Again, Nicolette was a godsend, easily hailing a cab for us and relaying the address Alec had texted me as we all piled into the back. The pub wasn't too terribly far, which I was grateful for; it was quite stuffy in the cab with the three of us squished together. We practically spilled out once the driver pulled up in front of the pub.

Automatically I glanced up and down the sidewalk in case Alec was walking towards us. There was no sign of his dark curls yet, so we headed inside and found a booth in the corner. I checked my phone to see if he'd texted, reminding myself that we were (surprisingly) early and I just needed to be patient.

As if I had conjured him myself, I suddenly spotted him entering the pub. His eyes scanned the crowd before landing on us, the corner of his mouth curling up into a smile as he began to make his way towards us. I gave a small wave, even though he'd already seen us, if anything to alert Sofia and Nicolette of his arrival. But it seemed I wasn't the only one who had noticed his entrance.

Nicolette was already standing to greet him, her arms held out, inviting him in for a hug. "Alec! So glad you're here."

He sent me a quick look over her shoulder, but hugged her all the same, albeit a little rigidly.

"Alec, that's Nicolette," I introduced her before gesturing across the table. "And this is Sofia."

Unlike our friend, Sofia stayed sitting and just sent him a warm smile and a wave. "It's nice to see you again, Alec.

Hopefully you won't run off on us again."

I gave her a quick kick under the table. Alec just looked even more out of place, but he managed a small smile.

"Aye. I hope I willna have to either," he nodded before slipping into the seat next to me. "I take it ye found the place easy enough?"

While his question was directed at all of us, his eyes landed on me last and lingered there. So I took it upon myself to answer and prayed the nerves were not evident in my voice. I somehow forgot just how handsome he was and it was slightly off-putting being so close to those warm brown eyes again.

"Oh, yes. It's not too far from our flat, so it was a fairly short cab ride," I waved my hand dismissively before smiling at him. "You picked a good spot."

That made him smile as well and not the tense smile he'd given my friends. Which of course just made me feel all warm inside. This was going to be a long night.

Alec

It took a couple whiskeys for me to loosen up, but the

girls made it easy. The one with the short hair that they kept affectionately calling Nic, had no problem carrying the conversation and not allowing for any awkward silences. While I was much more reserved myself, I could appreciate what her extroverted personality brought to the night. Lapses in conversation just made me recede even more, so I was grateful that there weren't many.

Sofia kept her in line, clearly the mother hen of the group. She made sure that no one ever had an empty glass in front of them; more than happy to wade through the crowd for refills.

It was different seeing Lydia with her friends. It seemed the drinks relaxed her as well and she would bless me with that beaming smile of hers often. And her laugh? God, I had no choice but to smile as well. She was radiant and I wanted to bathe in her rays forever. Okay, maybe that was a little melodramatic. Or a lot.

"So, Alec," Sofia spoke up as she set her glass down, dark eyes on me now. "Do you dance in the Scotland show full time or is that just a little side gig?"

"Och, no," I laughed with a shake of my head. "The dancing is just for spare change and to get myself out of the house. I'm an editor."

That piqued her interest, as well as Lydia's. "You didn't tell me that!"

"Did I forget to include that in my long story?" I asked,

smiling crookedly at the inside joke.

Lydia just nodded her head, eyes still wide. "Yes. You did. I mean...I know your Grandad used to be an English professor and you share a love of books, but–" Her lips pursed and her shoulders scrunched ever so slightly. "Well, I suppose that makes sense."

"I suppose it does."

She narrowed her eyes slightly at me, but her smile let me know that I wasn't in all that much trouble.

Nic inquired about what I was currently working on and I shared as much as I could. Of course, with the book being in the middle of the editing process, I couldn't give too much of it away, but I gave her the general idea.

"Do you have a specific genre that you prefer to edit?"

My brows pulled together as I traced my finger through the condensation on the table from my cup. "I'll edit most anything, but I do tend to specialize in historical fiction. I enjoy researching and helping the author fact check their information."

"Oh I just adore a good historical romance," Sofia gushed, clasping one hand to her chest.

"Every now and then a historical romance does cross my desk," I allowed, head ducking slightly as I tried not to glance at Lydia at the mention of romance.

After all, she had invited me out as a friend. She'd been very clear about that on the phone. We were barely a step above strangers. Though I couldn't help but hope that would change in the near future.

Lost in my own thoughts, I didn't realize that the girls had continued the conversation without me, comparing their opinions of the best romance novels which then led to romantic comedy movies and so forth. I was content to just observe the three of them (mostly Lydia) as I sipped on my whiskey. It was probably time that I slowed down. I didn't need to be completely sloshed before the night's end. Not the impression I wanted to leave them all with.

"Shit!"

I admittedly jumped a little at Nic's sudden outcry, quickly glancing around to see what could be the matter. Lydia seemed just as alarmed as me.

Nic looked around the table helplessly, "I forgot I have grades that I needed to submit by midnight."

"Oh, darn. Well, I'll go back with you and help. Don't want you traveling home alone," Sofia fussed, placing her hand on Nic's shoulder. She then looked at me and Lydia. "You two stay. You can bring her back to the flat, right, Alec?"

My mouth opened and closed like a fish for a moment as I looked between the three women before finally nodding my head. "Uh, yeah. Absolutely."

Lydia's brows were pinched together, but Sofia just sent us a dazzling smile and nudged Nic out of the booth.

The French woman stood and then took my hand in hers. I didn't yank it back even though the sudden touch took me by surprise. Not that I thought I could with how firmly the small woman was holding onto me.

"Oh, merci, Alec! You are an absolute angel," she gushed, her French accent suddenly thicker.

She wiggled her fingers at Lydia and blew her a kiss before disappearing into the crowd with Sofia. I was still trying to wrap my mind around what had just happened when Lydia began to laugh next to me, her face buried in her hands as she shook her head.

"Um. What was that?" I asked, even more at a loss.

She lifted her head and glanced in the direction her friends had left before back at me. "It was a setup. We don't have grades to turn in tonight. The kids barely have stuff to grade," she waved her hand. "Nic just thought she was being clever."

It took me just a few more moments, but then it all finally clicked and my mouth formed into what I was sure was a humorously perfect 'o'.

"I'm sorry. They're a bit eccentric at times. Especially Nicolette."

I noticed that her cheeks were fairly rosy. At least I wasn't the only one flustered.

"I think they're fun," I assured her, though she still looked at me skeptically. "Ye can tell how close the three of ye are. I'd never guess ye just met."

That made her smile, then, but the pink stayed in her cheeks. I just managed to see it before she ducked her head so her hair fell between us like a curtain. It was very tempting to brush it back behind her ear, but I resisted, instead wrapping my hand around my mostly empty cup.

"I'm very glad to have them. Last thing I wanted was to come here and be lonely," she admitted.

"Well no worries about that. From the looks of tonight, ye've got plenty of friends. Myself included."

She smiled at me then and sat up straighter. I was grateful she wasn't hiding from me anymore.

"I'm glad you came tonight," she confessed softly.

"Me, too."

The noise of the pub seemed to fade in the background as I gazed at her, easily lost in her sparkling, green eyes. I probably stared for too long as she suddenly averted her gaze with yet another blush.

But then she jumped a little and turned to face me, eyes wide. "Oh! I looked at the places you added onto my list and that cemetery sounds so cool! I didn't realize J.K. Rowling got inspiration for her characters' names from the gravestones there."

"Greyfriars Kirkyard," I nodded before glancing toward the windows. "Ye know it's not too far from here if ye'd like to visit."

Her eyes were as wide as saucers now. "Go to a graveyard? At this time of night?!" She was looking at me as if I was crazy, but I simply shrugged.

"Why not? It's always open."

"Because it's a graveyard. At night. That's creepy!"

"Why is that creepy?" I asked, my eyebrows pulled together in confusion. "People picnic there on their lunch."

I wasn't sure how much bigger her eyes could get without popping out of her head. It was quite adorable to see her so gobsmacked.

"You Scots are weird," she finally decided with a shake of her head.

"Why? Everyone there is dead. No one's gonna come after ye. Come on." I stood and held out my hand to her. "I'll show ye. It's really quite beautiful."

She gave me a look that reeked of skepticism, but she placed her hand in mine despite herself and scooted out of the booth.

Chapter 7

Lydia

I am an idiot. An absolute idiot. This was how I was going to die; at the hands of a stranger in a Scottish graveyard. It's like rule number one for girls when dating. Not that Alec and I were dating, of course. More like rule number one of being abroad, then.

But this was Alec! The man who took care of his grandfather and danced in a kilt in his free time. Also, he was apparently an editor. All of those are very innocent things. Sure, I may not know much more than that, but I'd never gotten any bad vibes from him and clearly my friends hadn't either or they wouldn't have left me alone with him.

Just to be safe, though, I quickly shared my location with Nic and Sofia. You know...just in case I didn't leave the graveyard.

Walking next to Alec, there were no red flags either. While he had initially held my hand in the pub, he let it go once we'd stepped outside and out of the crowd. He now walked comfortably next to me, pointing out places that we passed and giving some fun facts. It was easy to forget about our destination as I got caught up in his story of Edinburgh. I could understand why he enjoyed editing historical stories so much; he clearly knew a good amount of history. At least in regards to Edinburgh and Scotland.

He came to a sudden stop near an intersection where there stood a statue of a small dog on a pedestal above a drinking fountain, making him just about eye level. The small nose was golden compared to the dark coloring of the rest of the statue. Clearly he often received some loving nose rubs from visitors.

"Greyfriars Bobby," I read from the plaque.

"His owner, John Gray, moved here in 1850 and took a job with the police as a night watchman. Wee Bobby would follow him on his patrols. Then, when John passed, he was buried here in Greyfriars Kirkyard," Alec nodded across the intersection where I could make out a gate and the kirk behind it. "Bobby was said to have stayed at his owner's grave at night for fourteen years until he passed. Then they buried him in his own little grave. Visitors leave sticks at his stone."

The story was touching; that a dog wouldn't want to leave his owner's side even after they had passed. I couldn't help but reach up and give the good boy a little rub on his smooth nose.

"Are you just saying this to make me more comfortable

with going into a graveyard in the dark?" I teased, grinning at Alec over my shoulder.

"Aye," he nodded without missing a beat. "Wanted you to know that wee Bobby will be patrolling with us and keeping watch."

He sent me a charming wink before leading me to the intersection where we waited for the signal to cross safely. Needless to say, I was very surprised to find that we weren't the only ones here at this hour. A family was wandering amongst the tombstones and I could see a small tour group exploring the monuments further in the back. You'd rarely, if ever, see so many people visiting graves at night in America. Let alone a tour group.

"Scots don't have a fear of kirkyards like Americans do," Alec mused as if he'd read my mind.

We'd paused in front of the small tombstone that had been placed for the little dog, a pile of sticks in front of it just like Alec had described.

"There's just too many scary movies where bad things happen in cemeteries," I explained in an attempt to defend myself and other Americans.

He simply shrugged, "I think it's a peaceful place. Nice and quiet. People rarely talk here, or they talk quietly, and the majority of the people canna talk anyways." I scoffed and lightly tapped his shoulder with the back of my hand at that, but he just chuckled and continued as he began to walk along the path around the kirk. "Ye can come here on a sunny day and find a patch of green to sit with your thoughts and no interruptions. Which is a rarity in a city like this."

"Suppose that's what J.K. Rowling did?"

"Aye. She did some wandering around here when she needed inspiration."

I strayed just far enough from him to look closer at a low grave which had bars over it like a cage. I was so intrigued by the contraption that I wasn't exactly paying attention to where I was walking. Not the best idea when walking in a graveyard at night. One section of the path must've been just a little bit higher than the rest, because I caught my toe and suddenly I was lunging forward towards the grave.

Thankfully, Alec caught me before I could smash into the bars, one hand on my upper arm while the other grabbed my hip. He pulled me back upright with seeming ease.

"Whoa there," he chuckled, his breath warm on the back of my neck. "Didna mean for ye to go jumping into a grave. Maybe coming at night wasna such a good idea."

I just laughed, glad that it was nighttime, if only because the darkness hid the burning of my cheeks. Once I had regained my balance and some of my composure, I returned my attention to the grave.

"Why are there bars over it? Thought you said Scots weren't afraid of people coming back from the dead?" I teased.

"No, it's to stop people from getting in. Grave robbers specifically."

He then went on to talk about how there'd been a big issue of grave robbing after the Edinburgh University grew desperate for cadavers to dissect. People would dig up freshly buried bodies in the night and then sell them to doctors. In hopes of protecting their loved ones, some families had built these cages called mortsafes.

While the subject itself was not so great and quite dark, Alec's voice was very soothing as he recalled the facts. He shared them in such a way that had me hanging on to every word and wanting him to never stop talking. I'm sure my love of his deep voice and accent helped with that, too.

"Are you sure you shouldn't have been a history professor?" I asked with an amused smile.

He rolled his eyes. "You and Grandad are the educators. Not me. I couldna stand in front of a large group of people and give a lecture."

"But you can dance in front of a large group of people?"

"Och," he groaned, tilting his head back before leveling me with a look that I could see even in the dark. "It's no the same. Talking and dancing are two different things and the people that see me dance, I never see them again."

I just continued to stare at him, eyebrows raised, and had to fight back an amused smile. I don't think I did a very good job of it, though, because he let out a huge huff, his broad shoulders slumping a bit.

"You are a rare exception."

I just smiled smugly as he used his hand on my back to carefully guide me around the mortsafe and further into the yard. It hadn't gone past my notice that he had left his hand there after catching me and I wasn't about to complain either. I felt significantly more confident knowing he was right there if I needed him to save me again.

My eyes had adjusted to the dim lighting of the surrounding lamp posts and I was able to make out massive monuments and headstones built into the walls of the kirkyard. They were all extremely detailed and I could only imagine how old some of them were. Maybe I'd have to come again in the daylight hours.

I could hear another tour guide enter the kirkyard, telling the story of Bobby, but including how people claimed of seeing his ghost or hearing barking. I subconsciously walked closer to Alec's side at the mention of ghosts.

"You said Scots aren't afraid of kirkyards," I hissed under my breath.

He had noticed the group, too, and even though there

was an amused curve to his lips, he still directed us around them and back towards the exit.

"Do ye think those are Scots coming to hear ghost stories? They amp it up for the tourists," he explained.

While we had barely scratched the surface of the large kirkyard, I was grateful that we were leaving. Being an American, I could only handle a cemetery for so long, no matter how interesting.

"I know there's more to see, but it's quite dark now and getting a more busy. Maybe we can come back during the day time. The wee ghosties won't frighten ye then, eh?"

"I wasn't that scared," I faked nonchalance with a small roll of my eyes before nodding. "But yes. I would much prefer visiting in daylight."

He had dropped his hand at some point and walked over to press the button for the crosswalk so we could head back in the direction we'd come from. I followed after him, having to take an extra step for each of his big strides across the road.

"A cemetery—or kirkyard, I mean—is quite the interesting spot for a first date," I attempted a joke, glancing at him from the corner of my eye.

He stopped suddenly, his brown eyes a little wider as he turned to look down at me. I felt my stomach in my throat and struggled to swallow down the nervous lump. Maybe I had read this wrong.

"No. If I'm going to take ye on a date, it's going to be a proper first date."

I bit my lip to keep my smile from getting too big and goofy, but if this was going where I thought it was...

"Would ye like to go on a date?" he finally asked, one dark eyebrow raising unsurely.

"Yes," I nodded. "Absolutely."

The crease between his brows eased and now he was smiling just as big as I figured I was. "Absolutely," he repeated with his own nod. "Wonderful."

We started to walk again and I couldn't help the giddy feeling in my stomach. Alec waved down a cab for us and I gave the driver the address for my flat. It was only once we had started to drive that I realized my phone was buzzing multiple times in my pocket. Pulling it out, I saw numerous messages in the group text with Sofia and Nicolette.

Sofia

> What the hell are you doing
> In a graveyard??

> Lydia you better answer us
> right now!

Nic

> I swear if we left you with a
> serial killer, I will never
> forgive myself.

There were plenty of others with similar sentiments. Not wanting to stress my friends out further, I typed out a quick response telling them I was on my way back and would explain later.

"Sorry," I apologized, smiling sheepishly at Alec as I tucked my phone back in my purse.

"Friends checking in on ye?" he asked with a smile. "Suppose I have kept ye out fairly late."

"Yeah, they were getting a little worried since I hadn't responded, but I let them know I was heading home now."

Hopefully that would keep them appeased and from sending out a search party for me. Wouldn't put it past them.

Between the late hour and my flat not being very far, it took little time to get to my building which was quite disappointing. But then when I remembered we had a date to look forward to, I wasn't too terribly sad.

Alec leaned forward to speak to the driver before climbing out and holding the door open for me. I stepped out with a soft thank you.

"I asked him to wait while I walked ye to your door," he explained.

"Oh. That's very sweet of you," I smiled, properly pleased.

We walked side by side up to the door of the building and then paused, turning to each other. As usual, I didn't quite know what to expect from Alec and he seemed just as nervous as me.

"I'll reach out to ye about the date, then." He leaned down and placed a kiss to my cheek that made me grin with how sweet it was. "Goodnight, Lydia."

"Goodnight, Alec."

He made his way back down the stairs then and I watched as he walked back to the taxi, pausing before climbing in to send me one last charming smile and a small wave. I waved back, my own smile giddy, and then turned to key in the code and unlock the door.

I wanted to squeal and do a happy dance, I was so excited. I took the stairs two at a time, eager to get up into my flat where I could properly celebrate without anyone seeing or opening their door to tell me to shut up. Unlocking my door, I shouldn't have been surprised to find Sofia and Nicolette on my couch.

They jumped up as soon as I entered, their eyes wide as they rushed over to me.

"Thank goodness you're okay!" Nicolette cried, wrapping her arms around my neck.

I just laughed lightly as I patted her back. While Nic was relieved, Sofia was giving me a stern look, her brown eyes darker than normal.

"What the hell do you mean by sending us your location when he's taken you to a freakin' graveyard?! Nic had to keep me from calling the police and her only logical reasoning was your little dot was still moving around."

"I just wanted you guys to be able to keep tabs on me," I raised my hands in defense. "But really it was nothing to worry about. We just walked around and he told me different stories about the kirkyard. Honestly, the Scottish people just like...hang out in kirkyards as if it's a park. We weren't the only ones there."

"That still doesn't make me feel better," Sofia grumbled, arms crossed over her chest.

Nicolette had finally let go of me, so I walked over and wrapped my arms around Sofia instead. "I'm sorry for worrying you. Would it make you feel better if I told you that he asked me out on a date?" I raised my brows at her hopefully, trying to make my eyes as big and innocent as possible to butter her up even more.

Her jaw dropped, "Wait, he did?!"

Nicolette jumped up and down a couple times and clapped her hands together. "I knew it! Oh, I could see he was already head over heels for you. Just the way he looked at you tonight."

I think my cheeks were going to forever be stained pink from this man and sore from all the smiling.

"Well, I suppose I owe you a big thank you for ditching me to 'grade papers'," I gave her a look before softening it as I looked back to Sofia. "And I owe you big for worrying you guys. Next dinner night is completely on me and I'm spoiling you."

As hard as she tried to stay mad at me, I knew by the way she couldn't meet my eyes, that she was giving in. "And you're on coffee duty for the week," she added, side-eyeing me.

I nodded as I dropped my hands from around her to instead hold up my pinky. "You got it!"

Chapter 8

Alec

By the time I made it downstairs, Grandad was already up and sitting at the table with breakfast Orla had prepared for him. He held a steaming cup of coffee in one hand and the newspaper in the other.

"Mornin', Grandad," I greeted, placing a hand on his shoulder as I passed. "Smells delicious, Orla."

She looked up at me from her place at the stove with an affectionate smile. "Plenty of it if you're hungry, Alec. Your grandad has already had two helpings."

"I'll never have to worry about being underweight with Orla around," Grandad winked at his nurse.

I chuckled to myself and gratefully made a plate. Orla was quite the cook on top of being a great nurse and I would never turn down an offer of food from her. When I joined Grandad at the table with my own breakfast and coffee, he set down his paper and looked me over.

"Already dressed, I see. And where are ye off to?"

I felt my cheeks warm so I ducked my head a little, focusing on cutting the fried egg up. "I actually have a date today."

Grandad's bushy eyebrows rose in surprise. "Oi, are ye taking Amelia on a date then? It's about time!"

My chest panged and I shoved a forkful of egg into my mouth to hide my frown. Sometimes it was easy to forget Grandad's disease. Everything would be normal, but then he would mention something from years ago as if it was happening today. Amelia had been my long-term girlfriend of four years, but we had ended at least three years ago now. Seeing as how I hadn't dated since, I suppose I could see why that was the person Grandad remembered.

I gulped down some coffee in hopes of getting the egg past the lump in my throat, wincing at the burn. "No. Amelia is old news, Grandad. I'm going on a date with Lydia. The girl from the Scotland show. American?" I prodded gently.

There was a blank look to Grandad's blue eyes, making them look icy and distant. A man lost within his own mind. He blinked, though, when Orla practically dropped the spatula into the skillet and let out an excited shriek. We both turned to her in alarm.

"The one ye told me about? Oh, Alec!" she cried. "I told ye! What's meant for ye will no go by ye and here ye are, taking her on a date."

She fussed around with the stovetop a little, shutting off burners and adjusting the pans before her attention was completely on me.

"Now tell me all about it. What do ye have planned?"

"I was planning on a picnic at St. Margaret's Loch."

Orla's hands fluttered about and I could only be amused at how excited my date made her. Ever since she'd come to work with Grandad, I obviously hadn't had much in the way of a love life.

"Do ye already have your food planned out? I could whip something up easily for ye." She already began to move around the kitchen, checking the pantry and fridge to see what ingredients were available to her. "Little finger sandwiches, perhaps? With fresh fruit. Oh and we've got some teacakes or I could make ye shortbread in no time at all."

"I'm putting in a request for shortbread!" Grandad suddenly chimed in, making us both laugh.

"Grandad. You're not going on the picnic with us."

"Och, I know! But ye dinna need a whole shortbread just for the two of ye. Surely ye can spare some for your 'ol Grandad," he explained before sending me a charming smile. Who was I to turn down a face like that?

"Okay. Sandwiches, fruit, and shortbread," I allowed. "But I'll help ye, Orla. Don't want Lydia thinking I'm incapable of fixing my own picnic."

We got to work after I'd finished my breakfast and Orla had time to enjoy her own. I took it upon myself to work on the sandwiches and cut up pieces of fruit while Orla focused on the shortbread. Grandad hovered around, stealing nibbles of fruit or taste-testing the shortbread batter until Orla swatted him away.

"Why don't ye make yourself useful, Fergus, and find the picnic basket and a blanket?"

He rolled his eyes and grumbled something under his breath before following her orders and making his way out of the kitchen.

"Oh, I've already-" I shut my mouth as soon as the small woman spun to give me a look. She waited until Grandad had left and disappeared down the hall in search of the picnic basket.

"I ken ye probably already found it and brought it down, because you're a smart lad and I can tell you're excited for this date. But I canna handle him buzzing about like a bumble bee in a garden, sampling all the treats."

Another thing that was so great about Orla is she didn't put up with anything and Grandad knew that. She kept him in his place, much like Grannie used to.

I opted to take my own car to pick up Lydia and drive

us to Holyrood Park. While I wasn't the biggest fan of driving in Edinburgh, I much preferred the privacy it offered in comparison to a taxi. After asking her on a date, there was nothing I had wanted more than to hold her hand on the drive to her flat, but having the audience of our driver kept me from doing so. Which was ridiculous as I'm sure he'd witnessed far worse. The fact of the matter was I could still be painfully shy, even at my ripe age of thirty-five. You'd think I was fifteen by the way I acted around Lydia sometimes.

I managed to find a place to park near her building and made my way to the door to buzz up to her flat. It was only a few seconds before she answered.

"On my way down!"

I couldn't help but smile at the chipper tone of her voice. While it hadn't been that long since our night in the kirkyard, it felt like it. Working had suddenly become difficult when I had a date with a beautiful girl to daydream about instead.

My feet shuffled on the pavement as I waited for her, anxious and excited for our afternoon together. A flash of movement in the window caused me to look up and then the door was opening. I couldn't stop myself from looking her up and down. She was in a floral summer dress that flowed around her knees with a denim jacket over the top. Her hair pulled back from her face in a half-up half-down style again. It seemed to be her go-to, I noted.

"Hi," she smiled shyly, fair cheeks flushing a light pink. I loved when they did that.

My brain finally caught up and I stuttered out a "Hi" in response before clearing my throat and trying again. *Smooth, Alec.* I held my hand out to her in offering. "The park isn't too terribly far, but I figured we could take my car."

Lydia nodded as she placed her hand in mine. "A park date, then?" she asked with a coy smile.

I led her down the set of steps in front of her building and then turned in the direction of my car. "Aye. Figured ye may appreciate a picnic in a park more than a picnic in a kirkyard."

"And what gave you that idea?" she giggled.

I scrunched up my nose as I shrugged my shoulders before grinning at her. "Just a hunch."

I opened the passenger door for her, waiting for her to get settled in the seat before I closed it and rounded the car to get in behind the wheel. I caught a glimpse of Lydia looking in the backseat where I had stowed away the wicker picnic basket and blanket.

"Wow. We're having like a picnic-picnic."

"Are there other kinds of picnics?" I asked, pulling away from the curb.

"Any picnic I have ever been on is typically us stopping

at a gas station to buy snacks and drinks and then laying out a beach towel or something to sit on in the park. I don't think I've ever actually used a picnic basket or owned one, for that matter."

"Well if I am to take ye on a proper date, it's going to be a proper picnic."

Despite the nice, fall weather, the park wasn't too busy, which I was grateful for. Another perk of the tourist season dying down. I had grabbed the picnic basket and draped the blanket over that arm, leaving the other hand free should Lydia want to hold it again.

"I hope you don't mind a bit of a walk. Promise the view will be worth it, though."

Lydia paused in her appraisal of what she could see of the park from here and quirked an eyebrow at me with an amused smile. "This is already quite the view. I can only imagine if the one you have in mind is better."

I started towards the path and Lydia was right at my side in seconds. "If ye haven't caught on yet; Scotland is quite beautiful. Especially it's natural landscapes."

"Oh that was the first thing I noticed when researching."

We walked in silence for a while, enjoying the peace and quiet as we ventured further into the park. The only sounds were the crunching of the gravel beneath our feet and the wind rustling the tall grass and leaves.

"Did ye have a choice of which country ye taught in?" I asked curiously.

Lydia pressed her lips together, "Not really. I mean, I gave preferences, but I was fine with most anything in Europe. If I'm being honest, I was really hoping for something in the Mediterranean. Somewhere warm with nearby beaches."

"Instead, ye got the gloom and rain of Scotland," I chuckled.

"So far it hasn't been so bad and I find the sound of rain soothing."

"We'll see how ye feel in a couple weeks when rain is all ye hear and the sun hasn't shined in days."

Lydia playfully rolled her eyes as she nudged her shoulder against my arm. "I'll just stay cozy in my flat, then."

It was tempting to say something about being cozy together or invite her to cozy up in front of the hearth at my own home, but this was the first date and that was way too forward. Especially for me. So I just stayed quiet and relished in the warmth that spread through my arm at the lightest of touches from her.

There was no one else at the loch, so it was easy to find a spot to lay out the picnic blanket. Lydia helped by grabbing the other ends so the wind didn't blow it away and while I was quick to place the basket down, Lydia was quick to plop herself down on the other corner. Confident that the blanket wouldn't wander anywhere, I took a seat between her and the basket.

"Now I'll be honest with ye..." I stretched out my legs in front of me, feet hanging off the end of the blanket. "St. Margaret's Loch is a man-made loch."

Lydia gasped playfully, jaw dropping comically. "Oh, so you say you're taking me on a proper picnic date, but not to a proper loch?"

I just laughed with her and she shook her head before looking out over the water. She stretched her legs out next to mine and crossed them at the ankles as she leaned back on her palms.

"I still think it's beautiful," she mused.

And she was correct. The hills were still bright green, one last burst of color before they faded into their autumn hues. They were almost a perfect reflection in the loch below besides a few swans and ducks disturbing the water here and there.

"What's that?" Lydia asked eagerly, pointing to the ruins at the top of one of the hills.

"Saint Anthony's Chapel. Or what's left of it, rather. There's only two of its walls still standing," I explained.

"Can you go up and see it?"

"Aye. We can go after we eat, if ye like."

Her green eyes practically sparkled as she looked at me

and I knew it was a yes before she even said it. Speaking of eating, I figured I'd best get the food out of the basket. I turned and lifted the lid so I could retrieve the sandwiches, handing one to Lydia along with a water bottle. Then I placed the container of sliced fruit in between us.

"I also have freshly baked shortbread. Orla insisted on making something for us."

Lydia had started to unwrap her sandwich. "Orla is your grandfather's nurse, correct?"

I was honestly impressed she remembered. I think I had only mentioned her name in passing when we'd had tea together.

"Aye. She is also quite the cook and baker. Think that's why Grandad tolerates her bossing him around," I chuckled.

I regaled her with stories of Orla and Grandad's many tiffs as we tucked into our sandwiches. Conversation then morphed into Lydia sharing more about her life back home in Missouri and her childhood. All in all, it didn't seem too different from my own. Except she had been a good deal more outgoing than I had, being in her school choir and playing on the tennis team. I was doing good to wander outside the library doors.

Lydia was also an only child, so she seemed fairly amused by my stories of myself and Archie when we were little, green eyes locked on me as she smiled around a bit of fruit.

"So how did you get down from the tree?"

I rubbed the back of my neck. "Well, I—uh—more so fell from the tree. Archie and his friends grabbed a blanket and spread it out like you see in the cartoons. They convinced me they would catch me. However, the second I fell onto the blanket, I ripped it from their hands and hit the ground hard. Broke my collarbone, which gave Archie a good fright when I started screaming."

Lydia's eyes had widened so big I could see the whites of them completely around her irises. "Why would you ever think something like that would work?"

"It did in the cartoons," I shrugged before smiling amusedly and popping a grape into my mouth. "Needless to say, I stopped following around Archie and his friends after that. Kept to the safety of my books."

She laughed softly as she shook her head, looking back out over the loch. A pair of swans had drifted closer, dozing in the soft current with their heads tucked into their wings. It was a pleasant autumn afternoon.

I turned to place the empty Tupperware that had held the fruit back into the picnic basket and retrieved the shortbread.

"Orla baked an entire shortbread, but Grandad claimed half of it," I explained. "He would have taken more if he could, but Orla wasna havin' it."

Lydia looked curiously at the baked good, sitting up straighter so she could claim one of the precut pieces. She held one of her hands under the slice to catch any crumbs. I couldn't help but watch as she kept it poised there even as she took a careful bite. There was no avoiding crumbs when it came to shortbread, though. She giggled shyly at the small mess and then her eyes lit up a little.

"I've never had fresh shortbread before. I've only ever had the ones you buy in a box, but this is so much better!"

"I'll let Orla know. She'll be verra pleased to hear that."

"Please do."

I claimed my own piece and we both munched on the treats in silence until we had finished. We started brushing crumbs from our laps at the same time which just made us laugh again.

"I can see why your Grandad wanted to steal half of it. I could probably eat a whole one in one sitting without realizing it."

"Oh, he definitely has. His half is probably already gone by now and he'll be begging her to make more."

"Well, tell him I will join him for some shortbread and tea anytime if he'll have me."

My heart did a little flip in my chest. Even having only known Lydia for a fairly short amount of time, I knew Grandad would love her. They'd hit it off right away, whether shortbread was present or not.

"I'm sure he'd love to visit with a fellow educator. He's probably tired of seeing my face all the time."

Lydia gave me a small look. I was getting used to certain expressions of hers. "You've got a very handsome face, so I don't see how anyone could get tired of seeing it."

I had to fight hard not to blush, but it was very difficult. "Ye may be biased," I tried to tease. I then turned to make sure everything was packed into the basket. "So, what do ye say to walking up to the chapel ruins?"

Smooth transition, Alec. Definitely not obvious that you are changing the topic. Lydia went with it, though, and nodded eagerly.

"Absolutely!"

She was already moving to stand and waited until I had picked up the basket to help me fold the blanket. With just the tupperware and a plate in there, I was able to tuck the blanket into the basket and free up my hands a bit more. This time I took the leap and held my hand out to Lydia, palm up in offering. I didn't realize I was holding my breath until she had slipped her small hand in mine and gave it a tug as she started towards the path.

Lydia

The view from our picnic spot next to the loch had been absolutely gorgeous with the reflection of the hills and chapel ruins in the water, but the view from the ruins was just as beautiful with Edinburgh sprawling out in the distance. If I had to pick between the two, I don't think I could.

I kept a hold of Alec's hand as I carefully picked my way along the path to what little was left of the chapel. At least then if I repeated my fall I'd had in the kirkyard, he'd already have a hold of me. Fingers crossed we wouldn't have to test that out.

"This is stunning," I breathed, unable to resist reaching out to touch the stone wall.

Alec took a deep breath next to me as he looked out over the loch, a soft look in his eyes. "Aye. I'd have to agree with ye."

I could only imagine attending a service in the chapel before it had fallen to ruin. Surely, it'd be practically impossible to not feel God's presence when surrounded by his beautiful work. Scotland never ceased to amaze me with its natural beauty and I had barely scratched the surface. There was still so much of the country for me to explore.

"Do you want to take a picture?" I asked.

"Och, no. That's alright," he waved his free hand at me. "I dinna need a picture of me here. I'm sure my parents have plenty somewhere."

All I could do was laugh softly at his misunderstanding. "I meant a picture together. With me."

His cheeks flushed and he ducked his head a little to hide how flustered he was. I thought it was adorable when he got flustered, though.

"Oh. Well, of course. And I can take one of ye by yourself if ye'd like," he stammered out quickly.

"Yeah, I'd like that." I retrieved my phone from my purse and opened up the camera app while Alec set down the picnic basket. "Do you mind taking it? You've got longer arms than I do."

He chuckled, but took my phone anyway and held it out in front of us. Just as I expected, he was able to get both of us, the chapel, and the view in the picture with ease. I would've struggled for several minutes just to get us and the chapel.

With my heart hammering in my chest, I slipped my arm around his waist and was more than pleased to feel his large hand rest on the small of my back. That was something I could get used to. His touch was always sure and sturdy. So I felt more confident as I leaned into his side and got close for the picture, smiling widely at the camera.

Alec took a couple to be sure and then lowered his arm for us to check them. "Let me know if they're good and then I'll take one of ye from further back. Get all the ruins in."

I tried not to smile too big at the photo of us, it was just a first date after all, but I could feel my cheeks warm nonetheless. The sun was shining and Alec's eyes looked warm and bright. And his charming smile? First date or not, I clearly had it bad already.

"Looks great to me. Knew I could count on you," I winked at him to play it off.

He just chuckled and dropped his arm from around me so he could go back up the path with my phone. I looked around for a moment, unsure of what to do before finally deciding to stand in the open doorway in the one wall, the loch behind me.

Alec didn't take long to take the photo and then he was picking his way through the rocks back towards me, my phone held out to me in his hand.

"I have an idea," he smiled, taking his own phone from his pocket.

I watched him curiously as he swiped his thumb over the screen and tapped a couple times. My eyebrows furrowed even more when a Celtic song began to play. One that seemed oddly familiar, especially given I didn't regularly listen to Celtic music.

"Why do I feel like I've heard this song before?" I wondered out loud.

"It's the one I was supposed to dance with ye to. At the "Spirit of Scotland" show."

I looked up to him with wide eyes only to find him standing with his hand held out to me once more in offering. My stomach fluttered with butterflies as I placed my hand in his.

"Do ye remember the steps?" he asked gently as he stepped towards me.

"Very vaguely. I don't believe I did them correctly the first time around."

He smiled crookedly at that. "No worries. I ken them very well."

He moved to stand behind me then so our linked hands were poised above my shoulder. I at least remembered this part and held my free hand out to the side for him to hold in front of his chest. At some cue that he noticed in the music, he began to guide me through the steps.

My eyes mostly stayed on the ground at first as I tried to keep from tripping on a stray rock poking out of the dirt. Also to see what Alec was doing with his own feet and try to mimic it. The dance was repetitive, though, and I eventually grew confident enough that I could look up. Alec wore a pleased smile that grew even bigger when I locked eyes with him.

He lifted his arm for me to spin under and the skirt of my dress spun out around me. The ground was uneven and not being the most graceful, I started to lose my balance. Alec was quick to rescue me, wrapping his free arm around my waist and pulling me in tight against his chest. I just laughed which made him chuckle, too.

"Always having to save ye," he shook his head at me.

"Promise I did much better at the show. Granted the stage was flat," I explained with a giggle.

My heart was hammering in my chest and as I met his gaze once more, I knew it wasn't from dancing or almost toppling over. His brown eyes sparkled and I could feel myself falling. There was no stopping it.

"Alec. If you're not careful, you're going to make me fall for you," I warned, but my voice was soft and held no force behind it.

He just smiled even wider as he reached up to brush a strand of hair that had blown across my face back behind my ear. "Don't ye ken by now that I'll catch ye if ye do?"

Chapter 9

Lydia

There was loud, repetitive knocking on my door and I scrambled to dry my hands, glancing at everything on the stove to make sure it was okay before I left it to answer the door. I had barely cracked it open and Nicolette was already talking and stepping inside.

"Oh mon Dieu! I can't believe you've made us wait a full twenty-four hours to hear about your date," she huffed.

She was carrying a fresh bottle of wine and set it down on the counter to place her hands on her hips as she spun around to face me. Her raised brows suggested I had better explain myself. I was sure she'd start tapping her foot at me at any moment.

While Sofia was usually the more calm of the two, she looked just as expectantly at me, perching herself on the arm of the couch.

"Did you stay the night with him or something?"

My eyes widened and I quickly shook my head. "No! We just had our picnic and then he brought me back here. There was no staying the night with anyone."

I turned to the stove, grateful for the excuse to focus on something else and also hide the pink in my cheeks. The pasta was ready to drain and I turned the heat off for the sauce now that it was done simmering.

"Can I at least finish dinner and then tell you about it?"

Nicolette let out a displeased huff.

"Yes, of course. We've already waited this long and I'm sure it will be worth it." Even though I couldn't see Sofia, I could tell that she was sending Nicolette a look.

Nic and I were very different; she was extremely extroverted, energetic, and bubbly. I, on the other hand, was more laid back and controlled in my responses. Sofia was a good middle ground for the both of us and also much better at keeping Nic reined in when needed.

They both managed to be patient enough as I mixed together the pasta and sauce and then plated three dishes for us. Sofia joined me in the kitchen to retrieve glasses to fill with wine. We settled onto the couch with our food and drinks, Nic sitting cross-legged on the floor to eat at the coffee table. Unfortunately I had a feeling it would be a little while until I'd be able to properly eat.

"Okay. So I told you we were having a picnic. We went to Saint Margaret's loch and guys, the view was absolutely stunning." I pulled out my phone to show them pictures and smiled when their eyes widened as well, murmuring agreements.

"Oh that is such a romantic spot for a picnic," Sofia gushed.

I just smiled at the memory of it, still not quite believing I'd had such a wonderful first date. Quality dates had been difficult to come by in the past. This one had surely blown any date I'd been on out of the water.

"It was absolutely perfect. We chatted for hours while we ate and I got to learn more about him and his childhood. It was all very natural and I felt comfortable opening up to him."

It'd been like that even when he'd joined me for tea. Talking with Alec was just easy. I never felt judged and even if he didn't fully understand my experiences, he still made me feel seen. That was something I had been sorely missing the last few years, especially in my struggles with work.

When I looked at my friends, they were both looking at me with the biggest puppy eyes. Nic had even pouted out her bottom lip a little which just made me laugh.

"Just wait. It gets so much cuter," I assured her.

"How does it get cuter than a romantic picnic where you just get lost in each other?"

Sofia waved her hand at her to hush her, dark eyes never once leaving me. Clearly dinner and eating could wait. I told them about holding hands as we walked around the loch to the ruins and, of course, showed them the picture we'd taken together which just earned more fawning from them both. Then my favorite part.

"It literally felt straight out of some fairytale, dancing in the middle of the ruins with the sun shining. And then when he pulled me into his chest, I thought I was going to faint right there. His eyes are just so beautiful and up close like that?" I pretended to swoon and they giggled. "I knew I had it bad for him, but I tried to play it off and joke that he needed to be careful or I'd fall for him. And do you know what he said? 'Don't ye ken by now that I'll catch ye if ye do?'"

While my impersonation of Alec's accent was nowhere near the beautiful, deep gruff of his voice, it still caused Nicolette to literally squeal, her hands fanning excitedly in front of her.

"Que c'est romantique!"

"How on earth did you stay standing after that?" Sofia asked, just as wide-eyed.

"The only explanation is that he was holding me, because, my god, my legs got so weak when he said that." Even now, my cheeks were flushed and my heart raced as butterflies ran wild in my stomach. "We walked back to his car after that, still holding hands, and he brought me home. Then gave me the sweetest kiss on the cheek at the door."

"I would've never guessed he was such a cuddly teddy

bear with how tall and quiet he is, but he is an absolute sweetheart."

Sofia nodded in agreement. "I could tell that night at the pub. Yes, he's a big guy, but he was so calm and gentle. Especially with you. I knew he had it bad for you."

I knew my cheeks were still pink as I reached for my wine glass to take a sip in hopes of calming the butterflies in my stomach. But they hadn't stopped fluttering since my date, stirring anytime I thought back on it. Still holding my glass, I sank back into the cushions of my couch.

"It just felt so good to go on a date like that and with such a gentleman. It's been far too long."

"Dating has absolutely sucked recently," Sofia agreed, reaching for her plate to begin eating.

"Speak for yourself," Nicolette mumbled before stuffing a forkful of pasta into her mouth. "I've been on magnificent dates."

Now that we'd covered my date, it seemed we were all good to start eating. My pasta was still warm, thankfully. I had been worried it might be cold before I was allowed to eat it.

"Yes, but you've been on dates with women as well, not just men. The guys nowadays are just..." Sofia let it trail off, shaking her head at the lack of words to describe the current dating market.

Nic couldn't argue with that, so she just nodded in

amendment. "I will say the dates with women are typically more enjoyable, but every now and then I'll find a guy that's fun."

"I honestly don't think I've been on a date in over two years," I divulged.

It was a good thing Nic didn't have any food in her mouth at the moment, because her jaw literally dropped. "Two years?! And then you pull a beautiful Scotsman within just weeks of moving to Scotland?"

I laughed at that and then shrugged. "It just wasn't a priority. I was already giving my everything to my students and work. I barely had enough to give myself, let alone a significant other." It wouldn't be fair to someone else and I was not in the mental headspace for anything remotely romantic. Friendships were hard enough to maintain when I could barely get myself out of bed. "Add on that sex is such a big deal for a lot of people and not for me. It's been difficult finding someone who is okay with that."

"How do you think Alec will do?" Sofia asked gently.

I pressed my lips together and shrugged once more with a heavy sigh. It wasn't exactly something I liked thinking about. Especially when everything was going so well with him. Overall, I was in a better mental space than I had been just last month.

"I don't know. I'm hopeful he's okay with it, because I do really like him. But I also understand if he's not okay."

Nic frowned around the rim of her wine glass before setting it down decidedly. "Well if he isn't okay with it, then he's not the one. Onto the next!" she declared with a wave of her hand.

Sofia and I just giggled. Conversation wandered to other things now as we finished our dinner. Sofia made sure our wine glasses stayed topped off and it wasn't long before the bottle was empty.

Empty plates abandoned on the coffee table, we had all settled back into the couch. Nic had squeezed in between me and Sofia and was cuddling one of my throw pillows close to her chest. We were all full of delicious carbs and warm from the wine. Also a bit tipsy. However, I was a sleepy drunk so I just sunk further into the cushions and snagged one of my fuzzy blankets to curl up in, content to just listen to my friends.

"I think we should head out and let Lyds get some sleep," Sofia smiled over at me.

Nic followed her look and laughed softly, patting my knee. With that, they both stood and moved to take their plates and glasses to the sink. Sofia even grabbed mine.

"You don't have to clean up," I frowned at them. Yet I didn't move from the couch.

Sofia just waved me off anyways. "You cooked. We'll clean."

Not only did they clean the dishes, but the pans I had

used as well. All I could do was watch them with my bottom lip pouting a little bit.

"I love you guys."

Nic glanced over at me and then raised her brows at Sofia with a chuckle. With everything cleaned up, they made their way to the door, but paused to eyeball me.

"Don't fall asleep on the couch," Nic requested. "Please at least make it to your bed."

"I'm not that helpless," I laughed, removing the blanket from my lap just to prove it.

That seemed to satisfy them and they both called out their goodbyes before heading out the door. I forced myself to get up and lock it behind them, then shut off all the lights and headed to bed. Even with their teasing, there was still a content and happy smile on my face. Life in Scotland was turning out even better than I could have ever dreamed.

Chapter 10

Lydia

Returning to my classroom after dismissal, I still hadn't gotten out of the habit of being nervous about the mess I would find. It didn't seem to matter how many times I came back to things actually put away and a mostly clean floor. Years of returning to a classroom littered with broken pencil scraps, crayons, and stray tissues had left me dreading the end of the day. There was no way I could consciously leave the mess for the custodian to clean, so I'd spend a good twenty minutes picking up trash and straightening the desks back to their proper positions.

Thankfully, that wasn't the norm here in Scotland. My students were good about making sure all of their personal items were tucked away in their desks and any pencils that needed sharpening were placed in the dull bin at the back of the room, ready for my pencil helper to sharpen them in the morning during arrival. It sure made my afternoons easier and meant less time spent at work outside of contract hours, which was nice on days that I had plans after work like today.

Normally I would ride the public bus to our flat with Nic and Sofia, but I had plans to meet up with Alec for a quick dinner before his show. While he didn't perform as often as he had in the summer, tourists were still coming to visit Scotland for its beautiful auburn colors that littered the hills in the fall.

Content with the state of my classroom and feeling prepared for the next day, I grabbed my bag and flicked my lights off before closing the door behind me. It felt nice to leave the classroom and feel like I could leave work at work. That was a new feeling and one I could definitely get used to.

For the longest time, I hadn't been able to date simply because my life revolved around work and my students. Then my mental state was a mess after spending all day trying to control and de-escalate situations.

Now here I was, going on another date with a very handsome Scotsman after only being in the country for a month. Add on that I actually had the energy to go out and that made it all the more impressive.

While I had gotten better and more confident at navigating Edinburgh, I was still an avid user of my navigation app on my phone. Especially when going to a new place like the restaurant Alec had suggested. Granted I was an avid user of the app even back home.

The restaurant wasn't far from my school, though, and

I opted to walk. Edinburgh was never short of quaint storefronts that made any walk through the city interesting, never knowing what you might spot in a window display. It'd be a miracle if I didn't go home with twice as many things as I'd brought. Or more.

The window shopping was another reason I was grateful for my app and the woman's voice that would alert me when I needed to change directions. It was one hundred percent like me to get distracted by shops and get lost. (It had already happened a couple times since moving here). Not that I was in a hurry, anyways. I would beat Alec to the restaurant. He needed to wait for Orla to make it to the house, so I had the freedom to take my time.

My favorites were the little boutiques that displayed the most beautiful tea sets. Even though I still hadn't gotten used to drinking hot tea, I couldn't ignore the intricate designs painted on the delicate cups. I'd inevitably get one soon, it was just a matter of finding the perfect one. I'd drink water out of it, if need be, or hot cocoa this winter.

The book stores were a close second. As if I needed more books. I'd made the difficult, but smart, decision to only bring my Kindle with me. Books would've weighed down my suitcases in no time and I was already limited on what I could bring with me. Unfortunately, books just weren't as important as things such as warm clothing and toiletries. Go figure.

"Turn right in one hundred feet on Nicholson Street," the eerily proper voice instructed, breaking me from my thoughts.

I turned my attention from the store windows back to my phone, noting that the restaurant was just around the corner. I waited until I could see the sign before I ended the navigation and sent Alec a text to let him know I'd made it and would grab us a table.

Alec

I'm 5 minutes away. Be there soon!

I tucked my phone back into my purse and opened the large door to step inside. It was only a few moments before a hostess was greeting me.

"Is it just you or will someone be joinin' ye?" she asked sweetly.

"Two of us. He'll be here in just a few minutes."

She nodded and then waved for me to follow her over to a table. "I'll get ye a water while ye wait."

I thanked her and then reached for a menu, figuring I'd save some time by deciding what I wanted to eat now. Alec was on limited time after all. We were beating the dinner rush with an early meal, so I didn't have any concerns about us being able to get our food and enjoy it with plenty of time.

My attention had just wandered to the desserts menu when a shadow fell over the table and I looked up to see Alec. Instantly I stood up and wrapped my arms around his neck in a hug, having to stand on my toes to comfortably reach.

"Hey!"

His own arms wrapped completely around my waist and he gave me a gentle squeeze.

"Hi, there," he murmured, his deep voice muffled by my hair. We pulled back and took our respective seats. "How were the kids today?"

"Good!" I answered honestly, which was refreshing. "They got to be the teachers today and explained black pudding to me. I was not expecting it to be a sausage and when they first described it as a blood sausage I was very concerned."

There was in fact pork blood in the sausage, but I reminded myself I like my steak medium well and there's still blood in it.

Alec looked at me in amusement, his dark brows crinkling together and then one raising. "What did you think it was?"

"Pudding that was black. But I couldn't imagine what flavor a black pudding would be."

Now the wrinkle between his eyebrows grew even

deeper and I could see the gears turning. "What do you consider pudding?" he wondered.

"Well it's like…" It was my turn to frown in confusion. How did I describe what we considered pudding in the United States? "Like a custard, I suppose, and it comes in all sorts of flavors. You typically eat it in a dessert or from a little plastic cup when you're a kid."

Let's be honest, though, I one hundred percent still ate Snack Pack puddings as an adult. The butterscotch ones were a nice little treat and banana pudding as a dessert? Delicious.

"Aye, we've got pudding like that as well. I dinna think ye want black pudding in your dessert, though," Alec shook his head with a chuckle.

"Duly noted," I laughed as well.

Then the waitress appeared to take our orders and I was glad I had decided before Alec arrived, because I definitely had not even given the menu a second thought since he walked in.

Alec

Thank goodness I came to this restaurant often with my coworkers from the show, so I didn't have to quickly find something on the menu. Instead I merely ordered my usual, not even looking at the menu as I passed it back to our waitress. Our time was limited and I wanted to focus as much of it as I could on Lydia after not having seen her since our last date. Sure, we'd texted and even had a phone call at one point, but being face to face was different and much preferred in my book.

"So," she folded her hands together and rested her elbows on the table as she leaned forward. "What are your guesses for the tourists tonight? Older people again?"

"Och, one hundred percent. I bet ye two of the groups are older people and the last is a tour group from China."

"You are the expert, so there is no way I am betting against you."

"Smart lassie," I winked at her with a crooked grin.

It didn't go unnoticed that it made her blush a little. Add on that she averted her gaze. Lydia had very obvious tells when it came to getting flustered. Not that I could say anything as I was pretty obvious myself. At least it was fair between us, I supposed.

"Orla and Grandad say hello." In fact, Orla had

pestered me about when I would be bringing her over. She then went on a tangent about the dinner she could fix and I had slipped out of the house at that point.

"Tell them I say hello back. Oh! And did you tell Orla how much I loved the shortbread?"

"Yes, I did, and she promised to make ye more anytime ye want. Which made Grandad happy."

"In that case, I suppose I should request some soon so he doesn't have to wait too long," she giggled.

It was so easy to talk to her about Grandad. Others tended to ask how he was doing and the conversation revolved around his health and diagnosis. But not Lydia. She just went about conversation as normal and I appreciated it more than she would probably ever realize. It was nice to talk about him as if nothing was different from the man I had grown up with.

I knew that both Grandad and Orla would absolutely adore Lydia. It was hard not to and I couldn't imagine anyone having any ill feelings towards her. She just radiated warmth, even in gloomy Edinburgh.

We continued to chat with little to no awkward silences, even once our food arrived and we began to eat. I did mind my mother's warning to never talk with my mouth full and made sure I'd washed down my bite before responding to Lydia or sharing a tale. No matter how much she waved off my interest in her life, I found myself enamored when listening to her.

Thankfully, I had been smart and set an alarm on my phone warning me that I needed to leave for work. It's like I knew I would get distracted by her or something. The waitress had already brought over our check and I'd long since paid, so I suppose it was time.

"Would ye like to walk with me to the venue?" I asked hopefully.

I stood from my chair and held my hand out to Lydia as she pushed her own chair back. She smiled brightly at me and slipped her hand into mine.

"I'd love to."

We walked out of the restaurant and I steered her in the direction of the venue. It was only a couple blocks over which meant it was unfortunately a short walk. I wasn't quite ready to say goodbye to Lydia yet, so I paused outside of the back entrance marked with an 'Employees Only' sign.

"Ye could come see the backstage area if ye like."

She looked at the sign and then quizzically back at me. "Are you sure that's allowed?"

"Of course! Elize's boyfriend comes backstage all the time to bring her snacks and energy drinks."

She still didn't seem terribly convinced, but she didn't resist when I opened the door and gently tugged her inside. I was just grateful she hadn't noticed the comparison I made between her and Elize's boyfriend. Or she'd decided not to mention it. Obviously we weren't there yet, as we'd only been on a couple dates now. Though I hoped that we soon might be.

The hallway was narrow, so she had to walk behind me. There were a few doors scattered here and there for storage, tech, and the dressing rooms. Then the hallway finally opened up into the backstage area of the show.

The stage was currently lit up as the band conducted soundcheck and tech practiced their light cues. It didn't matter that the show was performed multiple nights a week, they always practiced to make sure everything was in order before guests were let in. The last thing tourists wanted was to pay big money for a subpar show.

"I've seen the show from the tourists' point of view, the stage view, and now the backstage view," Lydia mused, squeezing my hand a little. "I never imagined there'd be so much back here. How on earth do you keep from tripping on something in the dark?"

I chuckled, "Oh, we definitely have all tripped our fair share of times. It's quite dangerous back here."

The smile remained on her face as she looked around a little more. I didn't say anything, not that we could be heard above the band, and just guided her back to the hallway and the dressing room.

It was then that I first felt resistance from Lydia's hand

in mine whenever we approached the men's dressing room.

"Alec. I don't think I should go in there," she stammered, her eyes a bit wider than before.

I paused to turn to her and stroked my thumb over the inside of her wrist. Her heart rate had increased. "It's alright, hen. There's only three of us lads and they're always dressed by now. I'm not as punctual as them." To prove it to her, I rapped my knuckles against the door. "Are ye decent, lads?" I called out.

There were mumbled affirmations, but I still cracked the door and peeked in to make sure before opening it fully. Both men were sat in chairs by the mirrors, completely clad in their kilts and sporrans. They looked up as I stepped in and to the side to allow Lydia in.

"Graham. Hayden. This is Lydia. Lydia, this is Graham and Hayden." I nodded to each of the men in turn and they sent her a friendly smile and wave.

"Ah, so this is the Lydia we hear about all the time," Hayden chirped. "Are ye really going on dates with this guy after he ditched ye on stage?"

My jaw clenched and I fought the blush creeping up my neck. Though that was typically a losing battle. Lydia just laughed softly and gave my arm a light squeeze as she smiled up at me before turning her gaze back to Hayden.

"Cinderella ran out on Prince Charming and he still looked for her," she shrugged.

"Och! Does that make ye Cinderella then, Alec?" Graham giggled like a child, his hands literally holding his stomach as him and Hayden had a good laugh at that.

I glared daggers at them, but they couldn't see through the tears in their eyes. My next best option was to grab a discarded shirt next to me and toss it at them. It hit Graham in the side of the head and satisfyingly hung there until he reached up to yank it off.

Lydia was still giggling a little beside me, but at least she made sure to keep it mostly to herself unlike the two hyenas in front of me. I was even more grateful when she changed the topic and directed the attention off of us. Especially me.

"So I've heard that every family in Scotland has their own tartan pattern for their kilts. Are yours based on your families or just random ones the show gave you?"

Graham was pleasantly surprised and pleased by Lydia's interest, the smile clear on his face even as he looked down at his own kilt. "Aye. There are different tartans for Scottish surnames and clans. But, no. These are just random tartans they gave us so we match the girls we're partnered with," he explained before shrugging. "I'm sure it looks better on stage than each of us having a different pattern."

"Well I think it would be interesting to see a mix of tartans, but what do I know? I'm not a stage director,"

Lydia smiled back at him.

"Maybe you should become one."

"Oh, I don't think having an American woman direct a Scottish heritage show would be a good idea."

"Sounds like you know more Scottish heritage than you realize," Hayden winked at her.

Now it was her turn to blush and she ducked her head so a curtain of light auburn locks hid it from the other two. Thankfully I could still see the charming flush. She turned to face me, then, and again gave my arm a squeeze.

"I better get going so you can get ready, but I appreciate you showing me around. And it was nice meeting you both," she directed her last comment to Hayden and Graham who had calmed down significantly. Thankfully. I don't know if I could handle the next three hours with them teasing me like that.

"I'll walk ye outside."

Hayden and Graham bid her a farewell as I led her back out into the hall and in the direction of the back door. By the time we stepped outside, the sun was a good deal lower than it had been.

"Text me when ye get back to your flat, yeah?" I asked, worry creeping into my voice.

Lydia smiled reassuringly and nodded, "I will. Have a good show, break a leg, and don't let the boys give you too hard of a time. You're a catch."

She winked at me, which made me laugh. I couldn't help myself as I leaned down to place a sweet kiss to her cheek. I didn't have the guts yet to kiss her on the lips and just brushing against the soft skin of her cheek had my lips tingling. I could only imagine what a proper kiss would do to me.

"Goodnight, Lydia."

I let go of her hand and stepped back. If I didn't put space between us, I'd find a reason to stay out here with her all night. And I was definitely running behind already.

"Goodnight, Alec."

She sent me one more smile before turning and heading back to the main road. I watched until I couldn't see her anymore and then finally stepped back inside. Obviously I'd be checking my phone constantly as I got ready until I got that text from her, but I'd have to be nonchalant about it to avoid more teasing from the other lads.

Chapter 11

Lydia

"Twelve times twelve is…" the video on the Smartboard prompted.

My students replied with a raucous, "One hundred forty-four!"

GoNoodle had been a very useful site for me in my teaching career, especially on days when we were unable to go outside due to weather. It seemed Scottish children enjoyed it just as much as my American students had. All of them were standing and dancing or bouncing along to the beat as they practiced their multiplication. This was much more entertaining for them, and myself, than doing timed tests or worksheets. I really couldn't complain when it helped get some of their energy out as well. So long as we weren't bothering the surrounding classrooms.

When there was a knock on the door, I was worried it would be Mrs. Blackwood coming to complain and tell me to quiet my students. It surely wouldn't be the first time. With a deep breath to calm my nerves, I pulled on my big-girl panties and made my way across the room to open the door. However, I was greeted with a bouquet of wildflowers instead of Mrs. Blackwood's signature scowl.

"Hello, Miss Foster." Our secretary's head popped up above the bouquet as she lowered it. "These were just delivered for you."

My eyebrows furrowed in confusion, but I reached out for the vase anyway. "Oh. Thank you."

She sent me a sweet smile once she was sure I had a hold of the flowers and then bid me goodbye before disappearing down the hall. The video had concluded and now all of my students' eyes were on me as I carried the vase across the room to place on my desk.

"Miss Foster!" one of the girls gasped. "Those are beautiful. Who are they from?"

"Are they from your boyfriend?" another called out.

A couple boys made noises of disgust and I quickly waved my hand at them, attempting to dismiss the entire topic and hopefully avoid blushing in front of a bunch of pre-teens.

"You all are so nosy! Mind your business," I warned before giving them an amused smile. "How do you know Miss Dupont didn't send them to me?"

A few rolled their eyes at me, but there were still knowing grins. Thankfully they were distracted once more when I started a new video, this one a choreographed dance to N*SYNC's "Bye, Bye, Bye", despite having been nowhere near being born yet whenever the boy band was in their prime. If anything, they'd only know Justin Timberlake from Trolls. Now that was a sad thought.

Once I was sure that all attention was back on the board and not me, I picked the card from the flowers. The handwriting definitely was not Nicolette's; much less curly with sharp edges. A glance at the signature confirmed that it was Alec. Not that my students were correct, though. He wasn't my boyfriend. Yet.

I hope the wee ones are being kind to ye today. Thought ye could use some color during this gloomy week.

The bouquet was beautiful and just as colorful as he had suggested with soft purples and pinks. There were even a few light orange flowers scattered amongst the green. It was nice even just to see some green during this dreary fall. Edinburgh was already fairly dark with all the worn buildings being shades of brown, but now with all the greenery dying out and leaves falling, everything seemed to be in sepia tones.

I tucked the card into my purse to keep safe from prying eyes and adjusted the vase on my desk with a smile. The bell rang, pausing the students in their dancing and me in my thoughts.

"Time for lunch, everyone. Please line up at the door."

I paused the video to eliminate some of the noise as students pushed in their chairs and grabbed their lunches before joining the line. Even then, it was still quieter than I was used to. I was slowly adjusting to the new reality of teaching in Scotland and it was a welcomed change, that was for sure.

When I returned to my classroom to eat my lunch, I closed the door behind me to keep from being disturbed. Normally I ate with Sofia in one of our rooms, but I explained my little surprise and she was more than happy to give me some privacy. I didn't miss the knowing smirk on her face, though, as I continued down the hall to my own room.

Alec answered the phone on the third ring and I could hear the smile in his voice right away. "Well, hullo! To what do I owe the pleasure of your call?"

I rolled my eyes even though he couldn't see me. But there was still a smile on my lips; I was completely smitten.

"The flowers are beautiful, Alec."

"I'm glad ye like them."

"You stirred up quite the drama with my students, though," I teased as I gently dusted my thumb over the silky petal of one of the flowers. "I'm now going to have them all prying into my personal life even more than usual."

"I'd say I'm sorry, but..."

I could perfectly picture his smug smile and the easy way in which he'd shrug his shoulders.

"I considered sending some shortbread with it, but Orla isna here today and I figured the wee heathens would be hounding ye for a piece."

"Well I appreciate the consideration of that at least," I giggled. "I wouldn't get a single bite for myself."

Something about the relationship between teachers and students apparently gave them the idea that whatever was mine was theirs. That definitely would not be the case with Orla's shortbread. Every last bit of that delicious treat would be mine.

There was a moment of silence as I got my lunch box from under my desk, figuring I should at least get something in my stomach before the students returned for the rest of the day.

"How's your day with Grandad?" I asked.

"It's fine," Alec answered, the hint of a smile gone in his voice. "He's been cooped up in the library, which is nothing new. It's at least given me a chance to work on editing this novel. I've just got about a quarter of it left."

"And here I am interrupting you."

"Och, you're a lovely interruption," he insisted with a gentle chuckle.

Once again, I was grateful that he couldn't see me or the blush creeping up my neck. I took a bite of my sandwich, if only for an excuse as to why I couldn't respond.

"Do ye want me to let ye go? I'm sure you're on your lunch break."

"I am, but I decided to enjoy it alone in my room today," I answered, probably a little too quickly.

"Sofia isna eating with ye?"

I nibbled on my sandwich a little longer than necessary. "I may have asked her if I could eat alone so I could call you," I mumbled under my breath. But of course, Alec heard.

He chuckled once more in my ear, clearly pleased. "Now don't go making Sofia dislike me, because I'm stealing ye away from her."

If only he knew. Sofia would've shoved me into my room if I hadn't left soon enough for her liking. Her and Nic were the biggest supporters of my relationship with Alec. Our biggest shippers really.

"Oh, Sofia could never dislike you. You won her over

that night at the pub." And with every date he'd taken me on since.

"Even with taking ye to a kirkyard at night?" he asked teasingly.

"Okay, I will admit that made her pretty nervous."

Needless to say that I got little of my lunch eaten as we continued to chat. Like always, we got lost in conversation, one topic easily melding into another. I could have spent the rest of the day talking with him, but I did in fact have a job that I needed to do and a class full of kids waiting on me.

"Shit!" I cursed, almost dropping my phone when I saw the time on my computer screen. "I gotta go. The kids are done eating."

I was scrambling now to put my lunch away, knowing the kids would be waiting impatiently for me.

"Sorry to keep ye so long. I'll talk to ye later," Alec promised.

"Bye!" was all I managed to get out before I was dropping my phone into my chair and hurrying out of the room. While it wasn't the most sincere goodbye, it would have to do for now if I intended on keeping my job and staying in Scotland.

Just as I expected, all eyes were on me as I entered the cafeteria, my class the only one left in there.

"I'm sorry. I lost track of time," I apologized profusely

to the lunch staff.

"'Tis not a problem. The wee bairns have been perfectly behaved," one woman insisted.

Her thick accent and soft voice made me feel a little less anxious, even if the kids were still eyeing me with little smirks on their faces. They enjoyed me making errors, which happened quite often. Especially when it came to Scottish culture.

I nodded my head towards the hall and we made our way back to my room. The students all followed me silently until we got through the door and I had closed it behind me.

"Were you late because you were talking to your boyfriend?" the girl from earlier called out.

I just gave her my teacher look, gaze intent and eyebrows slightly raised. "What did I say about being nosy? You wouldn't like it if I shared all your secrets with the class."

Her cheeks flushed as a couple of her classmates giggled, but I knew I hadn't embarrassed her too bad. She was one of the students that could dish it out, but take it as well and I knew she appreciated my sarcasm.

The class settled back into their seats and I moved to the front of the room to begin the next lesson. Every now and then the flowers would catch my eye and I'd find myself smiling. The kids didn't tease me anymore about it and for that I was grateful. Nicolette and Sofia did enough of that already.

Chapter 12

Alec

"Oh, come on!" Lydia giggled on the couch next to me. "I promise it's really good!"

I just eyed her skeptically, but it was hard to keep up the stern facade when she looked so cute curled up in the corner. Her hair was pulled up into a messy bun, she was dressed in leggings and a college sweatshirt, and her makeup she'd worn to work had been scrubbed off before I even got to her place. Seeing this version of Lydia made my heart beat just as fast as it did when she was all dressed up for our other dates.

Her green eyes widened and her bottom lip pouted out as she looked at me. I just laughed.

"Lydia. Do ye really think I've lived in Scotland all my life and never seen an episode of *Outlander*?" I asked, raising a brow at her. She just looked innocently back at me. "I read all the books years ago."

Grandad had seen me reading them and it started a whole discussion on Scottish history, along with a long list of non-fiction books that I needed to read. My mother, on the other hand, had been the one who insisted I watch the show as well. Granted I believe we had very different reasons for watching.

Lydia's cheeks turned a charming shade of pink and those wide eyes flickered to her lap, then the television.

"We can put it on in the background," I insisted, not wanting her to feel too embarrassed. "At least, I ken what happens so I shouldn't get too sucked into it."

"You may have to keep me from getting distracted. Even if I have seen it," she admitted with a sheepish grin.

With that finally decided, she started an episode as I reached forward to grab the stack of papers closest to me on her coffee table. I blew a breath out as I looked over the rough handwriting of her Primary 5 students. Normally when I edited someone's writing, it was a typed up draft.

Lydia had her own stack of math assignments and I was more than glad to let her take over that aspect of the grading. Math had never really been my forte.

"How strict do I need to be in my editing?" I checked, eyes flicking over the top of the papers to Lydia. The students were only about eleven years old. The last thing I wanted to do was mark up their paper as much as I would a manuscript I was editing.

"I have a rubric somewhere."

Lydia scanned the coffee table, moving some of the papers around until she finally found it and held it up triumphantly before handing it to me. The requirements were simple enough. If anything, I'd be very picky about their grammar and that seemed an okay thing to be picky about.

We worked quietly together, the only sounds coming from the television and the scratching of our pens every now and then as we marked and scored our respective assignments.

Overall, I was fairly impressed so far by the writing of the students, given their age. That was until I came across one that had me wondering if I needed glasses. The child had chicken scratch for handwriting, to begin with, and the spellings of their words just did not make sense to me.

"What on earth does this say?" I asked, leaning over as I held the paper out for Lydia to take a look.

She finished up the problem she was correcting before leaning more towards me. She squinted at the page for a few moments before answering matter-of-factly, "My grandad went to the hospital."

I stared at the words for a few moments and then back at her, my eyebrows pulled together, looking at her as if she'd grown a second head. My expression must have been quite humorous because it made her laugh.

"What?"

"How could ye possibly get that from what they wrote?"

"It's a teacher thing," she simply shrugged as she sat

upright again. "Practically all of my students at my last school would write like that. I've only got a couple this year, but I've gotten pretty good at deciphering them."

"I'll say."

"You can put that one to the side if you want and I can look at it later."

I was torn between trying to prove my abilities and make another attempt at decoding the child's writing, and just letting it be and saving myself the headache. The latter won out and I set the paper between us so Lydia could look at it whenever she had the chance.

Any other misspellings I came across were simple enough for me to figure out and I was admittedly proud of myself for not having to ask Lydia for help. Which I then told myself was a bit ridiculous considering my career. It did go to show that teaching was no joke, however.

There was quite a pile of papers that she'd brought home and half of them had already been graded before I'd even made it over to her flat. She'd told me that this was just the work from this week. I couldn't imagine doing this every week for nine months. Teachers one hundred percent deserved their summer breaks.

The feel of eyes on me broke me from my thoughts and I looked over to find Lydia smiling softly at me. A blush crept up the back of my neck and it took everything in me to keep my eyes on hers instead of looking away.

"Is there something wrong?"

Lydia just smiled even wider and shook her head. "You're just really cute when you're concentrating," she answered bluntly.

Now I was really blushing.

"Thank ye, I suppose? Grandad said I always got a very serious look on my face, but I dinna think he ever called it cute."

"I may be slightly biased," she giggled with a shrug.

Then she let out a sigh as she looked around at the table in front of us. Somehow the mess of papers had seemed to have grown as we'd made piles of papers that had been graded, ones that I thought it best if Lydia checked over a second time, and the few left to grade. Thankfully.

"How does some tea sound?"

"I can make it," I offered, already standing up before she could.

"Do you not trust me to make a pot of tea? I promise I'm getting better," Lydia frowned playfully up at me.

"I'm sure ye can, but I trust ye to grade those papers more accurately than I do myself."

It was easy enough to find her kettle and the tea leaves in her small kitchen. There were only so many places for her to store them. I started boiling the water and then leaned against the counter as I waited, sneaking a look at

Lydia while I could without her noticing. She'd done the same to me, so it was only fair.

I found myself smiling softly as I watched her. Her grading pen rested against her lips as she looked over the assignment, the gears turning as she worked through the student's problem solving.

Even if she down-talked herself and had a history of struggling in the classroom, I could tell she was a good teacher. Amazing even. It was clear she cared dearly for the children, even after only knowing them for a few months. She wanted the best for them and that was the most any parent could ask for, in my opinion. I enjoyed the teachers who cared for me as a person more than the ones who fussed over my grades.

The kettle let out a whistle and I turned to move it from the burner so as not to disturb her. While I did my own tea up the normal Scottish way, I snagged a few cubes of ice from her freezer to place in Lydia's cup along with a couple scoops of sugar. While it wasn't an authentic sweet iced tea, it was much closer to her preference than my own cup.

"Here ye are." I carefully carried the drinks over and slowly bent to place them on the table, not wanting to spill anything on the papers.

"Thank you," she smiled gratefully. She picked hers up and was about to blow on it, but paused and looked at the cup in confusion. "It's not hot."

"I know you're not a big fan of hot tea, so I put some ice cubes in it to cool it off."

The smile she gave me about made my heart burst right there in her living room. It was blindingly brilliant and I hoped to make her smile like that often. My heart surely did burst, though, whenever she leaned over to give me a quick kiss on the cheek, the feeling of her lips burned into my skin even as she sat back.

"I'm sorry this is our date tonight. Not as exciting as our first couple dates, that's for sure," she mumbled after taking a sip.

I was shaking my head before she could even finish. "Don't be sorry. I'm just enjoying spending time with ye. I'm glad ye asked me to come over."

Thankfully she was blushing just as much as me now.

"I will say, this is the most I've enjoyed grading papers," she laughed softly. "It's nice to have someone sit with me. And when that someone is easy on the eyes, that helps, too."

She never ceased to amaze me with how quickly she went from shy and timid to confident and blunt. And always with that charming grin on her face like she knew what it did to me. It seemed I was once again winning when it came to the deepest blush.

"Lydia..." I shifted a little on the couch, setting down my untouched tea and then turning to face her. "I've been meaning to... I mean, I've been wanting to ask ye..."

You'd never think I was an accomplished editor and an English major with the way I struggled with my words around Lydia. I was as bad as the kid whose paper I was unable to read. But she just smiled at me encouragingly, just as patient as I'm sure she was with her students.

"I'd like to be exclusive with ye. To be your boyfriend, if...if ye'd have me."

She reached over and slipped her small hand into mine and I gave it a hopeful squeeze, my nerves calming a touch.

"I'd very much like that, Alec."

Now I was the one beaming, my grip on her hand tightening ever so slightly. An inner part of me was doing a celebratory dance, but I tried to remain as calm as I could on the outside.

Sure it may be foolish to start a relationship with a foreigner, but I was tired of always being so logical. Life had been difficult lately with Grandad's diagnosis and I'd honestly been quite down. Lydia had come in like the sun after months of rain and I didn't want to let that go; I wanted to soak up that warm sunshine she radiated for as long as possible. I deserved happiness, after all, didn't I?

"I will say, that's the first time anyone's asked me to be in a relationship with them right after I forced them to grade papers with me," she laughed softly.

Her thumb absently stroked along my pulse and surely

she could feel how rapidly my heart was beating. All I could do was laugh as well, feeling quite giddy if I was being honest.

"It definitely was not the papers that made me want to ask ye," I admitted. "And I wasna forced. I was more than happy to spend time with ye and put my editing skills to use if I could."

"I think my students may be quite proud to know that a proper book editor looked at their writing."

"Until they see the scores I gave them?" I raised a brow at her with a chuckle.

Her nose scrunched up and she grimaced a little as she tilted her head back and forth before laughing with me. I enjoyed how much time we spent laughing together. It was a stark contrast to the quiet of Grandad's home most of the time.

"Now Grandad is really going to want to meet ye. He's already pestered me about where I'm going each time I say I'm leaving for the night. And Orla, too."

"I've already told you I'd be more than happy to meet them. You just tell me when."

"I'll see how Grandad's feeling and let ye know the next time he's up for being social."

Lydia nodded understandingly and gave my hand a soft, gentle squeeze. Then her eyes were scanning over the table and she let out a big sigh as she sunk back into her corner.

"I think I'm all graded out. I'll finish this tomorrow during plan time or something," she reasoned with herself.

"I'd say you're good. We got a lot done."

She let go of my hand, only to organize the stacks a little. Then she was settling back into the couch, closer to me this time so that her legs rested against mine when her feet were tucked up underneath her. I allowed my arm to drape around the back of the couch, fingers brushing lightly against her shoulder.

"So do ye have any big sightseeing excursions planned soon?" I asked, remembering her list of places she wanted to visit during her time here in Scotland.

She nodded eagerly in response. "Sofia and I are going on a day trip to Loch Ness in a couple weeks before it gets too cold to be out on the loch. Then I really want to go to Midhope Castle where they filmed some of *Outlander*," she tipped her head towards the television.

I had completely forgotten about the show, too focused on trying to understand the writing assignments and too distracted by Lydia.

"Would you like to go with me?" she asked with a hopeful sparkle in her eyes.

"Of course," I answered with absolutely no hesitation. "Though I'm no Jamie Fraser."

She playfully rolled her eyes and lightly tapped the

back of her hand against my thigh. "I'd say you're better. Besides...I prefer dark-haired men over gingers."

She winked at me and I felt that infernal flush creep back to my cheeks. They'd permanently stay that way at this point.

"I think that is one of the highest compliments you could give a Scotsman in this day and age," I joked in an attempt to hide how flustered she made me. "You just tell me when and I'm there."

I'd have to make sure someone could cover any shows I had scheduled and more importantly make sure that Orla would be able to look after Grandad. Or maybe I could get Archie to come stay for the weekend. Either way, I'd find a way to go on a little getaway with Lydia.

She just smiled as she gazed at me and I found myself getting lost in her green eyes. I can't tell you if it was me or her who leaned in first or if a magnetic pull just tugged us both together at the same time, but before I realized it, her lips were brushing against mine. Taking the leap, I pressed my lips more fully to hers, reaching up to gently cup her cheek. I felt her lips curve against mine then and the kiss lingered for a few moments before she pulled away.

Her cheeks were tinted pink once more and I knew I had to have a goofy smile on my face. I'd been waiting a while to do that. My thumb brushed along the apple of her cheek.

"I'm glad I ran into you again that day," she mused, her voice soft.

"I'm glad ye invited me to join ye for tea," I countered.

Luck or fate, I was grateful for whatever it was that led me to her that day. To think I might have missed the opportunity had Grandad wanted something else or we'd had potatoes and I hadn't needed to run to the market. There was no sense going down that line of thought; we had gotten a second chance after I'd had to leave her at the show and now here we were.

Chapter 13

Lydia

They say healing is never linear. Despite that, a part of you still hopes that you might be the exception to the rule. I definitely wasn't.

In many ways, Scotland had helped me heal. Between my students, coworkers, friends, and Alec, I had been happier more often than not. Every now and then I'd have a down day, but not near as often as I had before this adventure started.

Within the past couple years, I had experienced depressive episodes that lasted months. I should've known I was on borrowed time here.

Thursday night I received a text from one of the teachers I'd stayed close with from my previous school asking me to call her. I naively thought she was just wanting to catch up.

"Hey! How are you?" I asked cheerfully once she answered.

"Hi, Lydia. I'm good." The tone of her voice made my brows furrow and I moved to sit down on my couch. "I just wanted to be the one to tell you. Devin's mother passed away last night."

My entire body froze, but my mind was racing, trying to make sense of what I'd just heard and what that meant.

Devin was a past student of mine from my first couple years of teaching. He'd always had a rough home life that often affected him in my classroom. There was a long stretch of time in which he would sleep the entire morning, completely knocked out in our calming corner to the point that I would have to gently shake him awake to go to lunch. Once he'd gotten food in him, he was set for the rest of the day and ready to learn. He just had to have his basic needs met first.

Then there were the times that a loud noise or a raised voice would trigger him and he would go running out of the room, body sent into fight or flight mode even if he knew he wasn't in any danger.

I did my best to care for him when he was with me and to help him with his academics so he could move onto the next grade. However, I still had stress dreams about him and what happened when he left the safety of my classroom.

"Wha—what happened?" I finally asked.

"Word is that she overdosed."

"And what about Devin?"

I knew that his father was long gone and it had just

been him and his mom since halfway through his fourth grade year. I didn't know of any other family nearby. Mom talked as if she had no one else to help when I'd voiced my concerns to her during conferences, what now seemed ages ago.

"He's been placed into foster care," she explained.

That didn't make me feel better. There was no telling what kind of family he'd end up with and if they would be prepared to handle his behaviors, let alone support him through this horrific event.

My mind continued to spiral with worst-case scenarios and jumped to wondering if he'd been the one to find her, to call for help. I didn't even register that I hadn't responded. What was there to say? Or to do, for that matter? I was a thousand miles away.

"Thank you for telling me," I finally managed, though my voice didn't sound like my own. It sounded distant and detached.

I believe she said something else, but it didn't register. At some point, one of us hung up, though I couldn't tell you who.

I struggled to sleep that night, tossing and turning, and my pillow case was damp from my random bouts of crying. The alarm clock on my nightstand mocked me as it ticked away, counting down the hours I had left until I needed to get up for work.

Work. Just the idea of going in and teaching today made my eyes sting. I was utterly exhausted, but my brain wouldn't allow me to sleep. There was too much to think about and worry about, even if it was completely out of my control.

I wished I had still been in Missouri; I could have fostered him. While I was not licensed as a foster parent, I had heard somewhere that teachers could get a temporary license in order to foster one of their students. Sure he hadn't been in my classroom for a couple years, but he would always be one of mine. They all were, no matter what. I would already have a relationship with him that might make the transition just the slightest bit easier.

My alarm finally broke me from my thoughts and I let out a groan as I turned over on my side to shut it off. I couldn't do it. I had gotten no sleep and I was a downright mess. Knowing my throat would be hoarse from crying, I just sent a text to let my school know that I was taking a sick day and would not be in. I copied and pasted it to Sofia and Nic as well so they didn't wait for me.

With that settled, I tossed my phone to the side and

burrowed back into my covers, begging for sleep to overtake me, but instead being greeted with another round of tears and sobs that I attempted to stifle unsuccessfully. I then cursed myself for being so ridiculous; it was not my own mother who had died and I was acting as if it were. But my emotions would not listen to reason.

The whole situation had thrown me back into the state of mind I'd lived in the last eight years, constantly worrying about my students and assisting them through the trauma they were experiencing. And in doing so, I had taken on their trauma as I tried to help shoulder the burden. Ultimately, trying to help and "save" everyone had been what destroyed my mental health the most and now here I was, falling into the same pit of despair I'd practically lived in.

As teachers, we put immense pressure on ourselves to help these students, not only become better learners, but better people as well. We get invested in them. The world tells us that we "change lives" and while it is a wonderful thought to think that I have the ability to affect a kid so much, it can also become an impossible standard to hold yourself to. Loki's quote, "I am burdened with glorious purpose" should be slapped on every teacher mug instead of those other cheesy quotes. It was far more accurate.

Despite my greatest efforts, I had not been able to change Devin's life. Not in the way that I so badly wanted.

In a way that would be truly meaningful and helpful to him. With his life completely upturned and his future so unknown, it was a hard thought to come to terms with. I was truly helpless in this situation and that made me feel like a failure.

It was yet another gloomy, rainy day in Edinburgh which made it difficult to tell what time of day it was or how much time had passed. I fell asleep at one point and was woken up by my phone buzzing several times. Most likely the school day was over and Sofia or Nic were checking on me to see how I was feeling. While I appreciated the concern, I currently couldn't fathom even typing out a response.

How did I explain that I had laid in bed all day, alternating between crying and sleeping, because of the passing of someone I barely knew? Even more so because I felt like I had failed a student and was questioning my abilities as a teacher, but ultimately because I physically could not get myself out of bed?

The mere idea of pushing the blankets back and sitting up was impossible. It required too much of me and right now I had nothing to give.

The rational side of my brain knew that this was too much. I was having a huge reaction to a small problem that wasn't truly mine. But that was the funny thing about mental health and depression; they literally did not care. Sometimes it took slipping on the tiniest of pebbles to cause a rockslide and send you stumbling back despite all the progress you'd made.

With the gloomy skies making my flat dark most of the day, I didn't notice when it became evening and then later night. The fact that I was in and out of sleep didn't help either. I couldn't look at my alarm clock to check the time, because I knew I would just feel guilty.

I told myself that I needed to just ride out this wave of depression instead of fighting it, allow myself to feel what I was feeling with no judgment. Easier said than done.

Not only did I still emotionally feel like shit the next day, I physically felt like shit, too. My muscles were sore from laying in bed for so long, my pajamas damp from waking up in cold sweats, and surely my hair was an absolute rat's nest from all my tossing about. Add on that I hadn't gone to the bathroom or eaten in over twenty-four hours and I was in an extremely rough state.

The one respite that came from my lack of motivation was the fact that my phone had died at some point and the notifications from it had stopped.

Faced with the possibility of actually wetting the bed, I finally slid out of the covers and shuffled into the bathroom. I didn't bother with turning on the light, not wanting to see my horrible reflection in the mirror. Even that small task, though, took it out of me and I slipped back into the bed and back to sleep. That was all I could manage to do.

The next time I woke up was to a knock on my door. The sound scared me at first, but then I let out a groan. It was probably one of my friends since I hadn't responded to any of their texts and with my phone dead, any calls of theirs would go straight to voicemail.

My assumption was confirmed when I heard a key in my lock and the door click open. At this moment, I was kind of regretting us all having keys to each other's flats. The last thing I wanted was to have them see me like this. Turns out I was wrong on both accounts.

It was a male voice that gently called out my name. A deep, Scottish accent that usually filled my chest with warmth. Now it just sent me into a panic. If I didn't want Nic or Sofia to see me, I definitely did not want Alec to see me this way. But it seemed I had no choice. His footsteps grew louder as he walked through my flat and then paused in the doorway of my bedroom.

"Lydia? Are ye awake?" he asked quietly.

Maybe if I laid still enough, he'd figure I was sleeping and leave. Who was I kidding? This was Alec. No, instead he just walked over to the side of my bed and gently settled down on the edge of it, careful not to jostle me. His large hand brushed back the tangled strands of hair from my face with a feather light touch and I grimaced at the feeling of pieces of hair peeling away from my clammy skin. I had no choice, but to open my eyes and look up at him.

"Oh, hen," he breathed out. "Are ye terribly sick?"

That look on his face was exactly what I had wanted to avoid from anyone else. The line of worry between his eyebrows as they pulled together, the tugging down of his lips, and god, that look of concern and pity in his eyes. His expression grew blurry, though, as tears sprung up in my own eyes. How I had any left, I really didn't know.

Chapter 14

Alec

Lydia had been cocooned in her duvet when I found her, the sheets completely pulled from each corner of the bed and tangled up between her limbs. Only her auburn hair peeked out of the heap and it was just as much of a disheveled mess. When she looked at me, her eyes were red-rimmed and the rest of her face was pale.

It was the look in her eyes, though, that had concerned me the most. It instantly reminded me of Grandad when he had just gotten out of an episode, his mind warring with the past and present and trying to come to terms with what was truly his reality. And then there was that fear in them; of what had happened and how little control he had.

I'd never seen this look in Lydia's eyes before, but I had an inkling of what it was. She'd never kept it a secret of how she'd struggled with depression in the past. While it was hard to imagine, given the lively Lydia that I knew, I also understood that the brain played by its own rules.

"Dinna fash, hen. I'm here with ye," I soothed, brushing back more strands of hair from her damp forehead.

Her eyes closed and a tear fell down her cheek, so I wiped that away, too. I was admittedly relieved, though, whenever she nuzzled her cheek into my palm, no matter how small the gesture. If I could bring her any comfort at all, I would be pleased.

I stayed quiet and used my free hand to begin the task of carefully detangling her hair. I worked slowly, being as gentle as I could. The last thing I wanted was to cause her any more pain.

By the time I had finished half of it, her breathing had slowed, signaling she'd dozed off. Her expression was more relaxed now, lips not as taut and the tenseness around her eyes gone. I was grateful she was able to find this small moment of respite and continued my ministrations. Once finished, I moved at the pace of a sloth as I stood and made my way to the kitchen. Anytime I felt bad as a child, my mother would always make me a cup of chamomile tea with biscuits. I knew Lydia had neither, so I donned my jacket once more and made sure I had Sofia's spare key to the flat before slipping out to visit the nearby market.

They had exactly what I was looking for and I snagged some other things as well that I thought Lydia might enjoy once she was feeling up to it. All in all, I was probably gone for only about fifteen minutes, but I still peeked into her room when I returned to check on her. She hadn't moved, so I contented myself to start on the tea, working as quietly as I could.

Of course, the kettle whistling was practically impossible to avoid and I winced as I quickly snatched it and moved it to another burner. There was the soft creaking of her bed and shuffling of her sheets as she apparently shifted, but it didn't last long and the flat was silent once more.

The sun was starting to set as I poured the boiling water over the loose leaves and I moved to turn on a couple lights while letting the tea steep. Then I placed a few biscuits on each saucer. My mother would've been proud of the set up.

Lydia seemed to still be sleeping when I carried the cups into the bedroom, setting them down on her nightstand before once again settling on the bed next to her. This time I gently rubbed my hand between the back of her shoulders, the blankets now draped carelessly about her waist. Her eyes blinked open and she took a moment to register her surroundings before meeting my gaze.

"I brought ye a cup of tea and some biscuits. It's no sweet iced tea, this time," I warned her. "I thought chamomile might be better suited."

Her gaze slid to the steaming cup next to me and then she was slowly moving up onto her elbow with a deep breath, as if the small movement took a good amount of effort.

"Thank you," she finally spoke, her voice raspy from lack of use.

I merely nodded and went to pick up the cup as she once again shifted, this time to sit up against the wall. She carefully took it from me and blew on it before taking a sip. Not wanting her to feel as though I was just watching her, I reached for my own cup and dipped a biscuit in before taking a bite.

After a few moments, long enough for her tea to cool, Lydia mimicked me and dipped one of her own biscuits.

"What do ye think?"

She chewed thoughtfully and took another sip to wash it down before she answered. "Fairly good," she allowed with a nod.

She merely nibbled on the rest of the one biscuit, leaving the other abandoned as she leaned over to set her saucer and empty cup back on the nightstand. Then she sunk into the pillows once more with a heavy sigh, but at least she stayed sitting this time instead of curling back up. That was progress in my opinion.

It was quiet as I finished my own tea and biscuits and I was pleasantly surprised when it was Lydia who broke the silence.

"Why do you call me 'hen'?" she asked, a curious crinkle between her brows. "Is it because my hair color is like a red hen?"

I chuckled softly as I set my cup down, shaking my head a little. "No. It's not that. Though you do have little feathers here and there that stick out sometimes," I waved my hand around her head at her sometimes unruly hair, but smiled affectionately to let her know I was only teasing. "'Hen' is just something we Scots call women. It's where ye get the term 'hen night' when a woman goes out with friends before her wedding. I don't think I realized I called ye it so often."

She shrugged, "Only a few times, but you've said it at least twice just since you've been here."

"I can stop if ye want me to or call ye something else."

She was quick to shake her head, one hand reaching out to rest on top of mine on the mattress. I couldn't resist turning my hand over to hold it.

"No, I like it," she insisted. "It's like 'honey', in a way, but shorter and sweeter. Though that could just be your accent."

Despite her current state, she still managed to give me a look that made my heart flutter and to shock me with her bluntness. I brought our hands up to brush my lips against her knuckles.

"Then I'll keep calling ye 'hen'."

Her eyes roamed my face and I kept my own eyes locked on her, taking in every expression or lack thereof.

When I lowered our hands, she moved them into her lap and lazily played with my fingers. At this point, I'd allow her to do anything she wanted, completely complacent.

At one point she opened her mouth to say something and then clamped it shut. Another attempt ended in only a huff. I just gave her hand an encouraging squeeze.

"How?" she finally asked.

While I wasn't sure what exactly she was asking, I could make my best guess.

"If ye mean how did I get in here, Sofia gave me her spare key." The why and the resulting how was probably more what she was wondering. "I hadn't heard from ye since Wednesday night, so I got a little concerned. But figured maybe ye just had a lot of work to do. It was when Sofia found my social media and messaged me, that I got more worried. She said ye called in sick yesterday and couldn't be reached.

I shrugged, "I suppose she figured maybe ye'd be more inclined to let me care for ye if ye were sick. Or maybe she didn't want to catch it and figured I didn't have an in person job to report to. Either way, she asked me to come and she met me at the door with her spare key to your place."

Her eyes never left me as I explained, but she frowned at the last part. "But you could've still gotten your grandad sick or Orla and I'd feel terrible."

I reached up with my free hand to tame down some of her hair that had grown frizzy on the side. "I had a feeling maybe ye weren't sick or ye'd have told me so yourself in a quick text. We may not have been together long at all, but I ken ye well enough."

She gave me the smallest hint of a smile, but managed to squeeze my hand more firmly. Her touch wasn't as clammy as it had been when I'd first arrived. Whether that was from the tea or the warmth radiating from my own hand, I wasn't sure, but I was glad for it either way.

"Do ye have a why? Or was it out of the blue?" I asked gently.

Her eyes got that far away look then as she gazed off towards the window. Today was just as gloomy as yesterday had been and all the days prior. It was just that time of year. I moved so I was sitting next to her against the wall and she leaned her body against my arm.

Lydia finally managed to tell me about her conversation with her old coworker. She also told stories of the boy and while some made her lips tug up into a small smile, more often they made her voice break around the apparent lump in her throat. Not that I could blame her; even I was heartbroken for the boy and I didn't know him from Adam. I struggled with my Grandad's disease, sure, but I still had him and my parents. Add on that I was thirty-four years old and well into adulthood. I couldn't imagine losing the last family member you had and at such a young age.

"I can tell ye care for the lad a great deal," I affirmed her before shaking my head. "But ye canna take on any guilt."

Even if Lydia had still been home in Missouri, he'd still have lost his mother and been struggling. Yet I knew that wasn't something she wanted to, or could, hear right now.

She just sniffled next to me, her head now resting on my shoulder. Now it was my turn to run soothing patterns along the palm of her hand with my fingers.

"Do ye have an address for him? Or an email? Maybe ye could reach out to check on him and show him that he still has people out there that care for him and support him."

"I don't know where he's at currently, but maybe someone could share with me his address once he's placed. I can always try his school email," she allowed.

I merely nodded and bent my head down to place a kiss to the crown of her head. "Sounds like a plan to me."

Suddenly, Lydia was sitting up away from me.

"I'm sorry. I probably smell horrible from spending days in bed and here I am all up on you with my greasy hair."

I looked down at her, amused at her concern. "I mean...I wasna going to say anything..." I joked. She narrowed her eyes playfully and that just made me smile even more. "Would ye like a bath or shower? I could change your sheets while you're in there. Then you and your bed can both be nice and fresh."

I could see a slight war behind her eyes, sure that she was going to insist I didn't need to do that, but thankfully she just nodded in the end.

"Thank you," she spoke softly. "That would be wonderful."

I waited until she'd gotten out of the bed and into the bathroom with a clean set of clothes before taking our empty cups to the kitchen. It was only once I heard the sound of the shower running that I fully relaxed and was able to start washing the cups. Then I set to work on stripping her bed and placing new sheets on it. Thankfully, Lydia had set them out when she'd gotten her clothes so I didn't have to go digging through her things. We definitely weren't anywhere near that stage of our relationship yet.

She took her time in the shower and I tidied up the rest of her small flat, hoping she wouldn't mind too much. I returned to her bedroom whenever I heard the water turn off and within a few minutes, the door was opening. While she was wearing comfy lounge clothes and her hair was wet, I still thought she looked beautiful. It was nice to see color back in her cheeks.

"How do ye feel?" I asked gently as she began to brush

through her hair.

She turned to meet my gaze and paused long enough to nod and smile at me. "Better. Thank you."

I merely nodded in return and leaned back on my hands to watch her, content with this little moment of domesticity. When she shut off the light and returned to the bedroom, she more closely resembled her regular self. Sure the dark circles were still there under her eyes, but her body didn't seem as weighed down as it had before, as if the entire weight of the world lay on her shoulders.

"What do ye say to cuddles and a movie or tv show?" I glanced over to the clock on her nightstand. "I can stay until about dinner time and then Orla needs to head home."

Lydia nodded and I stood to take her hand and lead her to the living room. It was probably good for her to get out of her bedroom anyways. The more she got up and moved about, the better.

Once I settled onto the couch, she curled up into my side and I draped one of her many fuzzy blankets over the both of us. Like a little kitten, she just snuggled further into my side, the blanket pulled up to her nose.

"Any preference?" I asked, reaching for the remote to turn on her TV.

"Something upbeat, please," she requested, her voice muffled from the blanket.

I found a romantic comedy that I figured she would like and wouldn't be too painstakingly cheesy for my own taste. At this point, though, I would watch whatever if it kept her mind occupied and her mood up.

Every now and then we would comment on the movie; point out a plot hole or how nobody would actually do that in real life. It was nice to hear her laugh, no matter how small it was. The shoulder of my shirt was completely soaked from her still wet hair, but I didn't care and hoped she wouldn't notice, because I knew she'd feel guilty. My goal was to keep that guilt at bay no matter what it was caused by.

The end of the movie timed out pretty perfectly, with me actually being ahead of schedule. As the credits rolled, I bent down once more to place a light kiss to her forehead.

"I best be going," I murmured, even if I didn't want to. "After I get Grandad all settled for the night, I'll text ye or you can call me if ye want."

Lydia sat up and I waited for her eyes to go to the dark, damp spot on my shoulder, but thankfully it didn't. Her eyes just stayed locked on mine.

"Thank you, Alec. I—" She let out a breath and shook her head, "I can't say thank you enough for everything you did for me today."

I just gently cupped her cheek and leaned in to give her a gentle kiss in response, knowing that brushing off her thanks would just upset her.

"I'll talk to ye in a bit," I promised. "Try and eat a little something for me, yeah?"

I raised my brows at her as I sat up straight and she bit her lip, but still nodded up at me. That was all I could ask for. We both stood and she walked me to the door, bidding me farewell before closing the door behind me with a click.

Chapter 15

Alec

Between Lydia's relapse and Grandad's health, it took a little while to find a time for them to meet. However, Lydia had been on the upswing the last week, seeming more like the girl I met at the end of summer, and it had been a couple days since Grandad had last had an episode. He was beyond excited to meet Lydia and constantly scolded me for 'keeping her away from him for so long'.

Orla was just as eager to meet her and had made quite a spread for dinner, insisting that she could stay long enough to meet her and chat for a while before heading home. I had a feeling she'd be here for more than just "a while".

"Alec, if ye could set the table. Dinner is just about done," she called.

"Already set it," I assured her, stepping into the kitchen. Of course she swatted me away from the stove when I tried to peek into one of the pots.

"Well then make yourself useful and check on your grandad. He's washing up."

Not wanting to get on Orla's bad side or put her in a mood, I did as she asked and headed for the stairs. Not that any sour mood of hers would last long once Lydia arrived. I wasn't the only one who could be affected by the warmth she exuded. Add on how excited Orla was to see me dating at all.

I found Grandad in his room standing in front of his full-length mirror. His bushy eyebrows were pinched together as he focused on knotting a tie around his neck.

"Well don't ye look spiffy?" I grinned as I stepped into the room. "Trying to show me up in front of my girlfriend."

He met my gaze in the mirror and I saw that tell-tale sparkle in his eyes.

"Och. I dinna need to dress 'spiffy' in order to show ye up. I'm a very handsome and charming fella. Where do ye think ye get it from?" he winked at me.

I watched as his weathered hands expertly maneuvered the tie, moving more from muscle memory than anything. The furrow in his eyebrows was simply due to Grandad's perfectionism. He always was meticulously put together. I suppose maybe the professor in him never left or maybe he'd just always taken pride in his appearance.

"Will ye get my sweater from the bed? I chose the blue and green patterned one to match her eyes."

Now it was my turn to scoff. "Oi, so ye are trying to steal her!" I teased.

I still moved to the dark wood, canopy bed to grab the sweater he had laid out. The wool was warm and albeit a little itchy, but he wouldn't notice through his white button up. With a thank you, he took the sweater and pulled it over his head. Then he was back to tugging and adjusting, his eyes scrutinizing as he looked himself over.

I simply sat on the edge of the bed and watched him as he moved over to his dresser for his comb; white tufts were sticking up here and there with static from the wool. But it was quickly tamed and he moved onto his cologne.

"I'm quite excited for ye to meet her, Grandad. I know you'll hit it off right away."

He turned and smiled at me. "I'm excited to meet the lass that's put that big smile on your face the last few months. It's been nice hearing ye hum happy tunes as ye go about the house."

My cheeks flushed a little; I hadn't realized I'd been doing that. I'd done it as a kid and would receive nudges from Grandad when my humming became too distracting from his own reading or writing.

He moved to stand in front of me and his fingers brushed through the mop of hair on my head. "I remember my hair used to curl just like yours. It was a devil of a thing to try and tame. My mam used to grease it down and the smell would make me gag."

"Well I'm glad my own 'mam' gave up on trying to tame

it long ago," I chuckled. "And messy curls are in now for men."

I didn't quite know that for sure, but no one made any negative comments about my messy hair and I often received compliments. Especially from women, jealous of the thick curls and wishing their own frail hair looked the same. If it meant not fighting with my hair, I'd take it. Also another perk of being a freelance editor who didn't have to worry about dress codes and such.

Momentarily lost in thought, I didn't notice the change in Grandad's expression, the sparkle dulled. His hand had dropped from my hair and he was looking about the room as if searching for something.

"The pearls. Your grannie will be wanting to wear her pearls."

He was moving to the dresser before I could register what he said, opening the top drawer and rifling through it while muttering to himself. A small lump built in my throat as I dealt with the inner battle of either explaining that Grannie would not be needing her pearls, or meeting Lydia for that matter, or playing along and acting as if everything were normal. Either way, the pearls were not here, having been given to my mother when my grannie was sick.

"She's already wearing them, Grandad." I cleared my throat when the lump was audible in my tone. "Ye know Grannie wouldn't leave the room without them if she was all dressed up."

His eyes met mine, a hint of franticness still in them as he glanced towards the door before slowly nodding. "Aye. Of course."

I stood up from the bed and held my arm out to him in offering.

"Why don't we go downstairs and wait for Lydia in the library? She's been dying to see your collection so I know she'll want to go there first." I leaned in conspiratorially, "Even if Orla's dinner smells absolutely divine."

The mention of books, the biggest constant in his life, was enough to get him away from the dresser and out the door. We made our way downstairs and I had just settled him into his chair by the hearth when I heard a knock at the door. My heart leapt in my chest and I couldn't disguise the smile that tugged at my lips. I hadn't even seen her yet and she was already making me feel lighter.

Lydia

I was in awe of the home even before Alec opened the door and revealed the interior. It was straight out of a novel or movie; exactly what you'd expect in Scotland. You didn't often see homes made of stone in Missouri and it gave the house a mystical feel, as if I were entering a cottage. You'd think after so many months here, the magic of Scotland would've dimmed, but it surely had not.

The large wooden door swung open and I smiled up at Alec who was already grinning down at me. Before I could say anything, he was bending down to wrap his arm around my waist and scoop me up into a sweet kiss hello.

"Well, hi," I giggled, admittedly quite flustered. But that's how I always seemed to be around him.

"Are ye ready for this?" his dark brows rose as he stood back upright and reached for my hand instead.

I just gave his hand an encouraging squeeze, causing his grin to grow, and he stepped back into the home. I followed after him, pausing in the entryway to take everything in while he closed the door behind us. The inside was just as cozy as the outside suggested with dark, warm colors throughout the two rooms I could see. A fire was visibly burning in the one down the hall, enhancing the homey atmosphere, and it was this room that Alec led me to.

My jaw may have dropped as I took in what was clearly the library that Alec spoke so often of. I could one hundred percent see why he and his grandad spent a majority of their day in this room. Shelves ran along an entire wall from floor to ceiling, absolutely jam packed with books. Some spines were more weathered than others and I could see many which were bound in genuine leather. Again...this place felt straight out of a movie.

Alec cleared his throat and there was movement by the fireplace. "Grandad. I'd like to introduce you to Lydia."

The elderly man stood from his large chair and turned, a finger holding his spot in his book. A wide smile broke from behind his white beard and I found it quite contagious. He stepped towards me and held his free hand out in offering.

"Fergus Morgan. It is very nice to meet ye, Lydia."

I felt almost as though I needed to curtsy given the setting and his apparel. Instead, I settled for just shaking his hand. His fingers were knobby, but his touch was warm.

"It's nice to finally meet you, Professor Morgan. Alec talks about you constantly," I glanced up at the tall man next to me. He'd let go of my hand at some point, probably so I could properly greet his grandad, and was instead resting it at the small of my back which I found quite comforting.

Mr. Morgan made a small face and waved his hand. "Och. Ye can call me Grandad if ye like. No need for this Professor Morgan. I retired years ago."

"I suppose I understand. It's weird to be called Miss

Foster outside of the classroom," I laughed shyly, brightening when he laughed as well.

"Aye. Alec did tell me that you're an educator yourself. Though I canna say I ever had a desire to teach the wee ones."

"You wouldn't be the first person to tell me that."

"Lydia is great with the little ones. She's always telling me about the creative ways she teaches them the material so they have fun with it," Alec chimed in.

I was surely blushing now at the praise. Even if Alec had never seen me at work, or even around children, I still appreciated the compliment knowing that it was completely sincere.

A woman appeared in the doorway with a wide and welcoming smile. I deducted that this was Orla, Grandad's nurse.

"Oh look at ye," she breathed as she stepped forward, arms outstretched for a hug.

I obliged, relishing in how soft and motherly it was. For a moment I thought of my own mother and felt a pang of longing. Then Orla was pulling back and cupping my cheek with one hand while the other brushed over my hair. Sofia had helped me take my usual chaotic mess of strands that weren't quite straight, but not curly either, and turn them into elegant waves that I could never have accomplished on my own.

"I can see why Alec was so taken by ye the night of the show." She smiled at Alec over my shoulder as if they shared a secret. Then her eyes widened apologetically and she met my gaze once more. "Oh, where are my manners? I'm Orla."

A laugh bubbled up my throat. "I just assumed you were. I hear that you take care of these two Morgan men," I nodded my head toward the two in question.

Orla smirked. "Aye. 'Tis both that I have to look after even if I only get paid to handle Fergus. I appreciate the recognition. Alec can be just as much of a handful as his grandad."

Alec made a disgruntled noise behind me that was somewhere between a grumble and a snort which made us both laugh. Then Orla was ushering us all into the dining room, insisting that dinner would grow cold if we continued to dawdle about. I was already in love with her.

She led Grandad through the doorway and into the dining room while Alec used his hand on my back to guide me along behind them. I slowed my steps so we fell back just a touch and leaned my head towards him to whisper.

"How's he doing?" I asked gently, glancing up at him. I noticed a shadow of something go across his face and the smile he gave me was very small compared to the usual one he wore.

"Okay. He had a little moment upstairs just before ye

came, but he seems to have moved on," he shared. His eyes turned to me then and his smile softened. "He said he wore that sweater to match your eyes."

It seemed that Alec wasn't the only Morgan who could flatter me and make me blush. I glanced over to Grandad as we stepped into the charming dining room.

"How did he even know?"

Now it was Alec turning red, his free hand nervously rubbing at the back of his neck. "I described ye to him after we had tea and I was late coming back with his breakfast."

"And he remembered? That was months ago."

"Mhm," he nodded, a proud smile pushing away the dark clouds I'd seen earlier.

I sat next to him with Grandad at the head of the table and Orla across from me. Right away she got to work on making a plate for Grandad, piling it high. A glance at him showed a hungry expression that reassured me he would be able to eat all of it. Not that I could blame him; Orla's food smelled absolutely delicious and if it was anything like the shortbread she had baked, I was in for a real treat. The table was full of comfort foods and nothing that looked too curiously Scottish for me.

"I hope that Alec told you how delicious your shortbread was that you made for us," I spoke up as I claimed my own share of the food.

"Aye, he did. I'm glad ye liked it so. I'd happily make ye

another batch anytime ye like."

Grandad's white eyebrows practically shot up to his hairline as he looked between me and Orla. "Sometime soon, hopefully?"

Her lips pursed and she gave him a look as she placed his plate in front of him. He was completely unaware, though, all of his attention currently on the food in front of him. He didn't hesitate at all to dig in and I was right there with him.

"Ye'd live off my shortbread if I let ye," she muttered.

"Happily," Grandad grinned at her.

Alec and I just chuckled and even Orla cracked a smile. I don't believe Grandad was one that you could stay upset with. He was an adorable old man and just as much of a charmer as his grandson, if not more. I could easily see why Alec loved him so much.

Conversation flowed easily as we ate and there was plenty of laughter. While I loved Sofia and Nic dearly, it was overwhelmingly enjoyable to participate in a true family dinner. There were times where I found myself just sitting back and listening to the three of them converse; mesmerized by the lilt of their accents, Orla and Grandad's thicker than Alec's, and entertained by their banter. Again, there was a pang of longing as I thought of my own parents back in Missouri. I really did need to be better about reaching out to them and checking in.

Obviously that had been a bit difficult with my mental state lately, as I struggled to communicate with anyone, and then add on the time difference. Had I been back home, it would have been my mother I ran to first for help and support.

A large hand giving my knee a light squeeze drew me out of my thoughts and I looked to Alec. His dark brows lifted slightly and I knew without him saying anything that he was checking to see if I was okay. I gave him a genuine smile and nodded. His eyes searched my face and then, apparently satisfied, he returned to the conversation, but his hand stayed on my leg. I don't think he even realized that he was gently rubbing his thumb along my knee cap. Unable to resist, I placed my hand on top of his and he instinctively linked our fingers together.

Orla stayed until dinner was finished, but Alec made her leave without cleaning up, promising that he would take care of it. She fussed a little about him cleaning up her mess, but finally gave in.

"It was so nice to meet ye, dearie. I hope to see ye again soon," she smiled warmly at me.

"It was nice to meet you, too," I returned the sentiment whole-heartedly. "Drive safe."

She bid the two Morgan men a goodbye and then gathered her things to leave. Alec began to collect his and Grandad's plates, so I picked up mine and followed him to the sink.

"You wash and I dry?" I offered.

He grinned at me as he placed the plates with the other dishes Orla had used to cook. "Ye've got yourself a deal."

I nodded and claimed a nearby dish towel, ready and waiting. Alec shoved his sleeves up his arms to keep them from getting wet and then dove right in. We made a good team, getting the dishes cleaned, dried, and put away before Grandad had even been able to finish his Guinness.

Alec grabbed another towel to dry his hands and turned to give him a look.

"Oi, so ye just sit there and watch us do all the work while ye enjoy your drink, eh?"

Grandad just grinned from behind his bushy, white beard. "I didna want to interrupt your little moment together," he shrugged.

Alec rolled his eyes and I just giggled. They really were quite the pair and I could see where Alec got his witty remarks from.

"Why don't ye show the lass around the house and I'll continue to stay out of your hair?"

"Aye, ye say that, but we'll see how long ye last."

Alec sent him a teasing wink, but placed his hand on my back once more and nudged me out of the kitchen. On the opposite side of the dining room was a doorway that connected to the front family room. The brown leather couch looked as if you could just sink into it and never come out. There was a visible spot at each end of the couch where the cushion was sunken in; obviously the preferred spots of the two men. I silently wondered which one was Alec's.

"Your typical family room, I suppose. Every now and then Grandad will come in here to watch TV, but more often than not, he's in the library," Alec explained as we passed through.

"I don't blame him. That library is so cozy, I could spend all day in there."

He smiled, "Well, you'd fit right in with us."

We made our way to the stairs then. They were somewhat steep and I wondered how Grandad managed on them. He seemed sprightly enough to me that I figured they weren't too much of an issue. Alec paused at the first door on the right and stepped in long enough to flick on the light before stepping back into the hall so I could see in.

"This is my room. Not much to it, though," he shrugged.

I wouldn't have guessed that he lived in this room if he hadn't blatantly told me. The walls were bare except for a few picture frames holding images of the Scottish countryside. There was a canopy bed and nothing about the bedding screamed Alec to me. It was all fairly aged and looked much more like a guest bedroom, which I suppose it was. The only sign of life was a bookshelf filled with books that looked much more recently published than those downstairs.

"Your personal collection?" I asked, glancing at Alec before I stepped in for a closer look.

He followed behind me. "Aye. Most of them are books I edited that I really enjoyed and then others are just some of my favorites in general."

I scanned the titles. While I was quite a reader myself, none of the titles really stuck out to me, but I had reason to believe that Alec and I had different tastes in books anyways.

"It's not much, but I've always been a minimalist so it's not like I had much to bring with me."

"Are you a mind reader?" I asked, smiling crookedly at him from the corner of my eye. He just smiled back.

"No, but I'm sure it's not the style of room ye'd think of a thirty-five year old man living in."

I could only laugh and nod. "I'll give you that."

Having seen it all then, I followed him back into the hall. He gestured to the room across from his, the light from his room illuminating it just enough to show a similar set up.

"Guest bedroom. Used to be my aunt's bedroom, so it's definitely girlier. Thankfully they kept my dad's old room less frilly," he joked.

I just rolled my eyes at him playfully, but followed along with him all the same. As in any house, there was a bathroom and then the master bedroom at the end of the hall. I couldn't hide my shock at the different items scattered throughout that clearly had belonged to Alec's grandmother.

A vanity held a cream-colored brush with soft bristles that would definitely make my hair frizzy if I tried to use something similar and an open jewelry box. On the chair was draped a purple, quilted robe that would keep you warm during the cold Scottish winters. Similar items sat on top of the dresser, including a photo that looked to be a black-and-white photo of the couple on their wedding day.

"How long has it been?" I asked quietly as if I might disturb the space if I spoke too loudly.

Alec matched my tone, however, it was most likely for a different reason. "Four years. She had cancer on and off for the last six and then it just spread too much."

Four years. It looked as if she had just been in the room this morning.

"She was a fighter, though. Ye'd never know she was sick by the way she acted. She'd tell me she had no time to be sick." A small smile made its way to his face, but there was sadness in his eyes as he took in the room. "They were quite the pair."

I carefully hooked my hand into the crook of his arm and smiled gently up at him. "I can only imagine. Your grandad is wonderful and I know your grandmother was just as amazing."

His eyes finally met mine again and his smile reached them a little easier this time. He covered my hand with his own, easily engulfing it, and gave it a small squeeze. Then he turned off the light and guided me back down the hall.

"He often forgets she's gone, so we've left her things as they were. It seems to help. Especially when he's just woken up," he explained.

It was easy to forget about the disease when talking to Grandad. I didn't notice anything different, but of course I'd only been around him for about an hour and he was still in the earlier stages. Orla and Alec were constantly with him and Alec had known him all his life, so any small difference was probably extremely noticeable to them.

I didn't know what to say. What was there to say? He'd lost his grandmother and was now slowly losing his grandad as well. All four of my grandparents were still alive, thankfully, so it was hard for me to imagine. When it was time for them to go, I could only hope that it was as quick and painless as possible. Not dragged out like Alzheimer's or six years of fighting cancer.

We returned to the library and I wasn't surprised to find Grandad back in the chair by the fire. The crackle of the wood was soothing and I felt better being in the warmth of the library, wrapped up in the scent of well-loved books.

Now that I wasn't nervous about meeting everyone, I could fully take in the room. It consisted mainly of two reading chairs on either side of a couch by the fire and two desks. One was piled high with stacks of various books and papers. The other was much more organized with only a laptop and a neat stack of papers that was most likely Alec's most recent manuscript.

"Can I know what your latest book is about or is it top secret?" I asked as I wandered towards the desk, grinning at Alec over my shoulder.

He chuckled and I was glad he was feeling lighter, too.

"I suppose it'd be fine if I told ye. Long as ye don't go blabbing to Sofia and Nicolette about it."

"I can trust Sofia to keep a secret," I scoffed. "Now Nicolette..." I shrugged my shoulders, crinkling my nose skeptically as I tilted my head back and forth.

We both laughed at that and then Alec stepped up to the desk. He neatly moved the pile of papers except for the last page which held the summary for the back cover. Up close I noticed that there were different colored tabs throughout the stack and I wondered what each color meant, but Alec was handing me the page before I could ask.

I leaned against the desk as I read the short summary, not surprised to find that it was a historical book. Alec had said those were the most enjoyable for him to edit. The plot didn't sound bad, though. In fact, it piqued my interest a little.

"Are you enjoying it?" I asked, holding the page out to him.

He placed it on the desk and then stacked the rest of the manuscript back on top of it, tapping the pile until it was neat and tidy again.

"Aye, it's a good tale," he nodded, crossing his arms over his chest and leaning on the desk next to me. "I've had to do a fair amount of edits and suggestions, though, so it's far from being published."

I eyed all the tabs once more. He clearly saw me, because I heard him chuckle softly and felt the desk shake under me from it.

"I'd explain my method to ye, but I believe it's more madness than method."

I raised my hands in the air defensively. "Hey, no judgment. That's exactly how my desk is at work. I know where everything is and that's all that matters."

A soft snore drew both of our attention to the hearth and I noticed that Grandad's head had lolled forward. I leaned forward off the desk and grimaced when the wood made a small groan.

"Suppose I should get out of here."

"I'll take ye home."

Alec carefully stood upright as well and instantly went to the foyer, already starting to slip on his boots before I could even say anything.

"You don't have to do that," I mumbled as I joined him. "I can catch a lift back. I carpooled with Nic here on her way to a date."

I was sure, though, that Nicolette would not be needing a cab back to our flat building. Most likely she would be staying with said date.

"Do ye not want to be around me anymore?" he teased.

My jaw dropped, "That's not it at all! I just don't want you to have to leave Grandad alone."

Alec glanced through the doorway back into the library. Grandad hadn't budged and we could still faintly hear his snores.

"Just let me get him up to bed and then I can take you. He'll be fine for the rest of the night."

It was clearly an "argument" that I wasn't going to win, so I merely nodded and started to slip on my shoes and coat. By the time Alec had coaxed Grandad out of the chair, I was ready to assist if needed. It turned out to be unnecessary, though, as Grandad was able to rouse himself enough to walk on his own.

Those bushy eyebrows tugged together when he saw

me and I could make out a small frown behind his beard.

"Och. You werena gonna leave without saying goodbye, were ye, Lydia?"

"I didn't want to wake you," I blushed. "But I can say goodbye now."

Without hesitation, I stepped in to hug him and smiled at the scent of wood smoke on his sweater, reminding me of camping trips with my family.

"Come over whenever ye like. We'd love to have ye," he smiled as he pulled back to look at me. He then jerked his head towards Alec behind him. "I ken this one would like that very much."

My cheeks flushed and I glanced over his shoulder to Alec. It was hard to tell in the dimmer lighting, but I had reason to believe that he was blushing, too. His smile was at least shy and he was quickly reaching for Grandad's shoulder.

"Alright, ye old bugger. Let's get ye upstairs to bed so I can get this one home to her own."

Grandad muttered something under his breath to Alec as they started up the stairs and based on Alec's response of lightly knocking the old man's shoulder, I had a feeling it was a good thing I didn't hear what he said.

While I waited, I texted Sofia to let her know Alec would be bringing me home. That was at least one friend she wouldn't have to spend the night worrying about. I'd just finished giving her a short summary of the evening when I heard footsteps coming down the stairs.

"Alright," Alec let out a breath, "He should be set for the night. He was already back asleep I think by the time I made it to the door."

He chuckled as he slipped on his coat and then held his arm out to me in offering. I didn't hesitate to tuck my hand into the crook of it. I was even more glad for his closeness as he opened the door and we stepped out into the cold, huddling into him more on the way to the car.

"I'll get the heat going as soon as possible," he promised, opening the passenger door for me.

Despite having lived here for months now, it still threw me off that the steering wheel was on the opposite side of the vehicle. The number of times I'd embarrassed myself by starting to the wrong side of his car were too many to count by now.

Once he'd closed the door behind me, he hurried around to his side and quickly hopped in. At least he found it to be chilly, too. I settled back into the seat, arms crossed tightly over my chest as I waited for the heater to kick on once he started the car. By the time we got a couple blocks away, I was able to loosen up more and took his hand when he offered it over the console between us.

"Your grandad is wonderful," I smiled at him. "I see a lot of him in you. It's no wonder he called you a miniature version of him. Though you're not so miniature now."

We both laughed and then he was raising his brows as he looked over at me.

"So are ye saying I'm wonderful, too?"

I scoffed lightly. "Have I not suggested as much before now? I feel like a bad girlfriend if I haven't."

"I'm just messing with ye," Alec was quick to shake his head, giving my hand a reassuring squeeze and stroking his thumb over the back of it. "I can tell Grandad is absolutely taken by ye. Not that I can blame him. I was fairly smitten myself when I first met ye."

Now it was my turn to blush, my gaze averting to the window so he couldn't see it.

"And Orla has taken a liking to ye as well."

"Well I've 'taken a liking' to both of them, so that's good to hear," I replied with a shy smile.

Tonight had been absolutely wonderful. I'd never felt so at home when meeting the family of a significant other, but it was hard not to feel that way with Grandad and Orla. Maybe it was just the Scottish culture, but I hoped that it was more than that. The last few months with Alec were amazing and I wanted it to continue that way. It'd been too long since a man had made me feel the way he did; so comfortable in myself and confident as well. In the grand scheme of things, we barely knew each other, but he had quickly become my best friend here and my biggest supporter. I could only hope that he felt the same in return.

It wasn't long at all before we reached my flat. Too soon in my opinion; I wasn't ready for this night to end. Alec found a spot to park in front before adjusting in his seat to face me.

"Can I walk ye to the door?"

I laughed a little, "Of course."

Not that I could imagine him letting me walk up there by myself, especially at night, but it was still sweet that he asked.

I climbed out of the car and tugged my coat tighter around me as I waited. Of course, Alec was quick to come around the car and wrap his arm around my shoulders to tuck me into his side. Again, I was grateful for his warmth as we walked up to the door, pausing just outside on the porch.

"I'm so glad ye came over tonight and I'm glad ye enjoyed yourself."

He was leaning down to give me a gentle kiss before I could even respond, his hand cupping my cheek to tilt it up towards his. I practically melted into his touch, leaning into him as I held onto his sides to keep myself braced. When he pulled away, I could feel those three sacred words on the tip of my tongue as I gazed up into his eyes, but I bit them back. I'd really be crazy if I told him I loved him now. It was too soon. Much sooner than I had ever considered saying them before.

"Text me when you make it back home, okay?" I asked. In some ways, that was the same as saying 'I love you', right?

He smiled and nodded, "Of course."

He waited as I punched in the code and only stepped off the porch once I had opened the door. I sent him one last wave as he backed down the sidewalk, waving back before turning to his car. The butterflies in my stomach and that tight squeeze around my heart didn't leave, even as I made my way upstairs and into my flat.

Chapter 16

Alec

By the time the show had ended, the temperatures had dropped drastically and the precipitation was more sleet than rain. All of us had the hoods of our coats up as we hurried to our cars, managing small waves and shouts of 'drive safe' before we were ducking behind the wheel. I rubbed my hands together while I waited for the car to heat up. Hopefully the roads wouldn't be too bad and Orla would be able to make it safely home after I relieved her of her duties.

Once my windshield wipers had cleared the slush on the glass, I carefully pulled out of the lot and made my way home. For the most part, the roads weren't bad, or at least any worse than usual. There were just a few slick spots here and there, but thankfully everyone was driving carefully.

Orla's car wasn't parked outside of Grandad's house when I got there. I didn't blame her if she had decided to head home early to beat the weather. Grandad was probably already in bed and wouldn't be needing any assistance anyways.

I was wrong on both accounts.

While the living room was dark when I entered, light poured through the doorway to the kitchen and dining room. I could also see a fire burning in the library, though the flames were low. Then I heard two voices, one of which was definitely Grandad and the other of which was definitely not Orla.

I was more than surprised to find Lydia sitting at the table with Grandad, a Scrabble board spread between them. Based on the amount of letter tiles on the board, they had been at it for a while.

Lydia was just finishing up placing the last tile of her word when I stepped through the doorway. She turned towards me, her face lighting up.

"Hi!" she smiled widely, standing to greet me with a hug.

While I was still a little gobsmacked, I managed to wrap an arm around her in return.

"Hello, hen. I didna expect to see ye here."

She pulled back and glanced towards the clock. "I didn't realize it was so late," she looked at me sheepishly. "I meant to text you to let you know you didn't need to rush home, but I guess we lost track of time."

I looked over her shoulder at my Grandad who was just grinning at me. Not that I could blame him; I'd be grinning too if I'd just gotten to spend the last few hours with my wonderful girlfriend.

"I was feeling a bit homesick after work, so I thought I'd come spend some time with Grandad until your show was over. I insisted Orla go home early to beat the storm and she fought me on it, but I finally won out."

"She's a stubborn lassie when she wants to be," Grandad chimed in. "Which is saying a lot knowing how stubborn 'ol Orla is. A mule, that one."

"Och. And look who's talking."

It was no secret how mulish he could be and Grannie had easily matched him. Of course, they always gave in to each other in the end.

"I suppose I'll take that as a compliment?" Lydia eyed him skeptically before laughing.

She took my hand in hers and led me over to the table. I sat next to her and looked over the board, impressed by some of the words they had managed to create. Grandad had always been an avid Scrabble player. No surprise there.

"I will admit, though. I made a grave mistake agreeing to play Scrabble against an English professor," Lydia grimaced.

"Och, ye've been doing great."

"If you say so."

I couldn't do anything but smile at the two of them. I

knew they'd get along well and this little moment I'd stumbled upon just proved it. They bantered as if they'd known each other for years; Much like myself and Lydia. It made me feel warm inside to see her fitting so comfortably into my life and amongst my loved ones. My heart might burst if I ever got to see her around my nieces.

"Looks to me as if ye've been giving him a pretty good run for his money," I mused, eyeing the board appreciatively.

"I think the both of you are just sucking up to me."

She grinned at each of us in turn, but her smile softened when she looked at me and I instinctively reached out for her. Her hand found mine upon her knee and she easily interlaced our fingers as she looked over the letters she had.

"How was the show tonight?" Grandad mused.

He laid out some of his tiles to spell a new word; tactile. Lydia sure was brave for taking him on. He and I could spend hours upon hours competing and arguing over whose words were real or not.

"Quite entertaining. Hayden pulled up a lady who could barely make it up the stairs without tripping on her own two feet. The whole partner dance just turned into a jumbled mess of people, but they all seemed to enjoy it nonetheless."

Lydia managed to find another word in her jumble of

letters and set out the tiles before jotting down her points on the notepad. I couldn't tell from here who was winning.

"Well, it's a truly great show. I feel like the stumbling over each other just adds to the fun of it," she shrugged.

Grandad took a moment, his brows pulled together so they almost looked like one fuzzy caterpillar on his forehead while his fingers stroked at his beard in thought. Those sharp eyes of his darted between the board and his letters again and again before he finally laid a couple out.

"Damn. I was hoping you'd finally get stuck," Lydia huffed. She let out a sigh as she turned her holder around to show Grandad her lack of options.

His eyebrows relaxed and he beamed at her. "Aye, but it's all about the points, dearie. What did we end up with?"

Lydia quickly added up their points, her teacher brain solving the math much faster than I could've done. I peeked over her shoulder to see. Even though she'd gotten some high scoring words, Grandad had snuck in some of those letters that scored him big points.

"Three-hundred eight for me and three-hundred forty-two for you."

Despite losing, she still smiled widely at Grandad who held his hand out for a shake. "It was a well matched game, lass. I enjoyed a challenge for once."

His smirk was directed towards me this time, making me roll my eyes, and Lydia just giggled next to me. Then he busied himself with putting the letter tiles back into the velvet bag.

"I'll clean this up. You go and enjoy each other's company," he mumbled, nodding his head over his shoulder without looking at us.

Despite his words, Lydia still gathered up a good amount of the tiles and dropped them into the bag when he held it out to her with an appreciative smile.

"You two take care of that and I'll fix us some chamomile tea." It was late and the last thing I needed was caffeine keeping me awake. Grandad surely didn't need it either. "Would you like a cup, Grandad?"

"I wouldna mind a cup before bed. Thank ye, laddie."

I let go of Lydia so that I could get up and head to the kitchen, turning on a burner while I filled up the kettle. Then I retrieved three cups from the cabinet and placed a bag in each so they'd be ready to steep as soon as the water was hot.

It wasn't long before Lydia was joining me. I jumped a little at the feel of her arms wrapping around my middle and her head resting just below my shoulder blades, surprised at the intimate gesture. A glance over at the empty kitchen table suggested Grandad had moved on to either the library or his bedroom. The clock above the stove read ten-forty-five. It was well past his usual bedtime unless he was really lost in a book he was reading. Even then, he was usually dozing off in his chair and I'd have to rouse him to get him up to bed.

"Did I scare you?" Lydia asked with a giggle, her voice slightly muffled against my sweatshirt.

"Well I definitely wasna expecting it," I chuckled in return before resting one of my hands over hers. "But doesna mean I don't appreciate it."

She just gave me a gentle squeeze in response before letting me go as the kettle began to whistle. I poured the boiling water into each of the three cups and then turned to face her, my hands falling to her waist.

"Would you like to go cuddle on the couch? We can put on something if ye like while we drink our tea or just chat."

Lydia nodded, "Sounds lovely. I'll take our cups in there while you take Grandad's to him."

Without waiting for a response, she carefully picked up two of the cups and made her way through the doorway into the living room. The light switched on a few moments later. I grabbed the other cup and slowly made my way to the library so as not to spill any of the hot liquid. One singular lamp was left on and the flame in the hearth had died to embers. No sign of Grandad which meant he must've headed upstairs.

I found him in his room, sitting in the armchair by the window. He looked quite pensive and I was nervous as to where his mind would be, but the look cleared up whenever I knocked my knuckles against his door.

"Alec. There ye are." He held his hands out as I approached him and carefully took the tea cup, just cradling it in his hands for a moment. "Thank ye, laddie. I appreciate it."

"Of course, Grandad." I bent down to place a kiss to the top of his head. "Just call for me if ye need anything, otherwise I'll bid ye goodnight."

His hand reached out to find mine on his shoulder and gave it a squeeze, his touch warm from the tea.

"She's a keeper, that Lydia." He looked at me with a soft smile, his eyes sparkling. "Reminds me of your grannie."

I felt my eyes begin to sting and blinked back any threat of tears. My smile was still a little shaky, though.

"Aye. They're both wonderful women. We Morgan men have good taste," I winked at him to lighten the mood.

He laughed heartily at that and gave my hand a pat. "Aye, we do."

Then he dropped his hand and lifted the cup to take a tentative sip. Deciding that was the end of the conversation, I let him be, an odd feeling in my chest; warmth at the idea of Lydia being like Grannie, but also a chill from missing her and thinking about the enormous loss Grandad must still feel.

The warmth only grew, overpowering the sadness,

when I made my way into the living room and found Lydia curled up in a corner of the couch, legs tucked under a blanket she had found. Typical Lydia. She was probably disappointed in the lack of blankets we had in comparison to her. I knew the only reason it wasn't currently pulled completely up to her chin was because she needed to be able to hold her cup of tea.

She smiled over the rim at me and then lifted the end of the blanket in offering.

"Ye look very cozy," I noted as I joined her.

I didn't even bother with my own cup; I just sat and gently hooked my hand around her far thigh to pull her legs across my lap and her body closer to mine. She didn't protest, instead just smiling pleasantly to herself as she carefully adjusted the blanket around us both and then settled her mostly empty cup on her lap.

"Well I'm extra cozy now," she grinned up at me.

I felt like I was sinking into her deep, green eyes. I didn't even know if she had turned on the TV. My body was exhausted and happily sunk back into the couch with her soft weight grounding me further. However, my mind was running a mile a minute.

"What?" Lydia giggled softly, a shy smile on her face. I must've been staring too hard. "What's that look for?"

I opened my mouth and then closed it again, probably looking like a gaping fish. How did I put it into words?

How I felt after finding her here when I returned home and seeing her with Grandad. And then Grandad's sentiment upstairs.

"You're very special, hen, and I just can't get over how lucky I am to be with ye."

Her cheeks really turned red then and her chin ducked down towards her chest. I noticed her thumb stroking up and down the handle of her cup before her eyes were on me once more.

"I wonder the same thing about you. It all seems too perfect to be a coincidence that we met. And then met again," she added with a laugh.

It felt like fate that I found her that day on the way to the market. Sure there'd been a good amount of attractive women that had come through the show, but nothing came of it as I was a) not one to just hand out my number to random women and b) smart enough to know that many of them weren't staying long. Then I'd left her on stage, sufficiently ruining any opportunity to talk to her further. Yet, the world had given us a second chance that neither of us took for granted.

I reached up to brush an auburn lock behind her ear and let my hand rest at her cheek as I leaned in to kiss her. Her lips met mine, soft and loving as she let the kiss linger. Even when she pulled away, she moved just far enough to rest her forehead against mine, noses still brushing.

"Whatever it may be, I'm grateful for it," I murmured softly. "For everything that led ye to Scotland and to me."

Chapter 17

Alec

I had heard of Thanksgiving before, but only had a vague understanding outside of it being an American holiday. Needless to say, I had never celebrated it, having never been to the United States before. Lydia reassured me that nowadays it was mostly just about enjoying time with family and friends and eating a bunch of delicious food which all sounded wonderful to me. I would never be one to turn down a feast.

Sofia was the one hosting it in her flat, being the only other American besides Lydia, and had encouraged everyone to bring a dish that meant something to them. I had opted for my mum's cullen skink, a hearty soup filled with smoked haddock, potatoes, and leek. Absolutely nothing could beat curling up on a cold, wet day with a bowl of cullen skink. It would warm you all the way down to your toes.

Lydia met me at the door of her flat building and held it open as my hands were full with the large crockpot. I still managed to bend down enough to give her a quick hello kiss which made her giggle.

"Ye look very cute and cozy," I commented with a smile.

She was wearing a burgundy sweater that complimented her auburn locks and black jeans. Her blush didn't go unnoticed, even though she turned to head to the stairs, obviously trying to hide it from me.

"Thank you. So do you," she sent her own shy smile over her shoulder at me.

We made a pit stop at her own flat to get the dish she had prepared and then made our way down the hall to Sofia's. With both of our hands full, I had to use my elbow to knock on the door, which just made Lydia giggle. Thankfully Sofia was quick to answer and beckon us in.

The smells of food baking in the oven and on the stove top hit me as soon as I stepped in. I was very curious to see what everyone else had brought, never being one to shy away from trying new foods.

"Here, Alec. You can plug that in over here if you need to and Lydia there's pot holders you can place underneath yours on the counter."

Always the organized one, I was not surprised by Sofia's pre-planning and did as she suggested, setting the crock pot onto the counter near the wall so I could plug it in and keep the soup warm.

The flat was very similar to Lydia's except that Sofia

had decorated in warmer tones of beiges and browns with some pops of color here and there. Nicolette was sitting on the couch with a curly-haired girl I didn't recognize. Based on the fact that they were holding hands in Nicolette's lap, I assumed that this was the girl she had been going on dates with as of late.

As if she read my mind, Lydia was at my side, her hand coming to rest on my arm.

"Alec, this is Cassandra. Cassandra, this is my boyfriend, Alec," she introduced.

The woman's dark eyes turned to me then and she smiled brightly. "This is the famous Alec, then. It's so nice to meet you. You can call me Cass."

"Oh no," I chuckled nervously. "Why am I famous?"

"I told her about you ditching Lydia on stage," Nicolette shrugged, but there was a mischievous grin on her face.

Lydia and I seemed to sigh in unison. I could feel her chest rise and fall with a huff against my arm.

"He did not ditch me, Nic. It was an emergency."

Nicolette merely shrugged at the correction and went back to whatever she had been talking to Cass about prior. Cass just sent me a conspiratorial smile before returning her attention to Nic. Obviously she was used to her antics by now.

"Don't worry, Alec. You won't be the only guy here," Sofia reassured me as she stirred something on the stove top. It looked like rice, but it was a reddish-orange. "One of our coworkers is coming. Another fellow Scot, too, so there'll be three of you versus us three foreigners."

"Och, you're all honorary Scots to me," I grinned at her which caused her to grin back.

Lydia led me over then to the couch so we were out of Sofia's way. Turns out Cass was a local Scot as well, having grown up in Edinburgh, though her parents were originally from southern England. Once she said it, I could hear it in her accent which was an interesting blend, but still easy to understand.

She was quite the contrast to Nicolette with her fair skin and light brown hair cut just below her chin. Cass, on the other hand, had chocolate-colored skin despite the lack of sunlight as of late and while her tight curls came just below her collarbones, I could only imagine how long it was when wet. But the lass had no problem keeping up with Nicolette's fiery personality and they really did make quite the adorable couple, sending each other googly eyes every now and then.

I wondered if Lydia and I ever looked like that. I sure felt like I did sometimes; a goofy smile on my face and probably the most lovesick look in my eyes. It was hard not to look at her that way, though. She was absolutely wonderful and I'd never felt so comfortable around a woman straight away. Even with having "ditched" her the first time we met.

The other lad, Brian, arrived fairly soon after we had and Lydia introduced him to myself and Cass. He was one of the upper grade teachers, specializing in mathematics. While that wasn't exactly my area of expertise, we had other similar interests that kept conversation flowing until Sofia announced that dinner was ready. She didn't have to tell any of us twice. Everyone was off the couch and to the kitchen at the mention of food.

Ever the teacher, Sofia quickly took control of the small bit of chaos and brought everyone's attention together. "Okay, before we start filling our plates, I'd like everyone to explain what they brought."

"And do it quickly. I'm starving," Nic called out, earning a shush from Lydia and a nudge to the ribs from Cass.

Sofia just eyed her in that motherly way of hers, then she started us off by revealing her chicken chimichangas and spanish rice, both making my mouth water. Nic had been in charge of dessert and had made crepes with a variety of toppings for us to choose from. I explained my soup and was pleased to see that Brian had brought scotch pies. While Cass was Scottish born, she had brought a traditional African dish called Muamba de Galinha.

"What's in it?" Brian asked, curiously leaning forward to get a better look at the dish.

"Chicken and okra cooked in peanut butter."

Then it was Lydia's turn.

"Well mine doesn't have a fancy name. My family just calls it cheesy goodness," she giggled shyly. "But it's hashbrowns, chicken soup, sour cream, and cheese with corn flakes on top for a nice, sweet crunch."

"Cheesy goodness?" I grinned down at her, keeping my voice low.

She shrugged sheepishly. "Maybe it'd sound better in another language, but that's what we've called it ever since I was little."

Show and tell time over, Sofia allowed us to fill our plates. Then we all piled onto the couch, balancing our plates in our hands or laps. I'd gotten a little bit of everything to try, but after just a few bites, I knew I'd be going back for seconds, if not thirds. Thankfully, I wasn't the only one.

Lydia stopped much sooner than I did, so on my last trip, I took her empty plate to the sink. When I returned, she was reclined back on the couch, her hands placed on her full stomach. I smiled at the sight of her and carefully sat down, not wanting to jostle her. As soon as I was settled, she was wiggling closer to me so she could rest her head on my shoulder with a content sigh.

"Going to fall asleep on me, are ye?" I smirked before taking a bite of food.

"It's called the post-dinner nap. It's a Thanksgiving tradition," she mumbled. "Everyone stuffs themselves and then finds somewhere to doze off in the living room."

"A feast and then a nap? Now that is my kind of holiday."

She grinned at that and just nuzzled her head further into my upper arm. If she wanted to nap, I was more than happy to be her pillow.

My current plate was not as full as my last few, so it didn't take me long at all to finish it. Not wanting to disturb Lydia too much, I simply leaned forward and placed the empty plate on Sofia's coffee table for the moment, promising myself I'd put it away soon enough. When I leaned back, I lifted my arm and without a word, Lydia adjusted to lay her head on my chest while I settled my arm around her shoulders. I couldn't resist placing a soft kiss to the top of her head, even if we were surrounded by four other people. I couldn't see her face, but she gave me a gentle squeeze around the middle in return.

"We forgot to share what we're thankful for," Sofia suddenly blurted, her dark brows pulled together in a frown.

"Do ye have to do it before ye eat?" I asked.

"I suppose it doesn't matter."

"Let's do it now, then," Nicolette shrugged. "I'll go first! I am thankful for...wine and my friends."

We all laughed at her insistence on including her favorite beverage of choice, not at all surprised. But her affectionate smile towards Sofia and Lydia in my arms made up for it.

"I am thankful for my job," Cass chimed in.

"I am thankful for breaks from school," Brian decided with a laugh, which the other teachers nodded adamantly in agreement to. "Winter holiday cannot get here soon enough."

It was Sofia's turn. "I am thankful for getting to share this holiday with you all and experience delicious foods from different cultures."

It was my turn and I took a deep breath, not a fan of having all eyes solely on me. There was a lot of pressure to come up with something good and everyone else had mostly taken anything that I would've said. A glance down at my girl still curled up against me made it extremely clear what I was most thankful for.

"I am thankful that I ran into Lydia again and that I get to be here with all of you."

That earned a couple of 'aww's from her friends, but I was more focused on the look on Lydia's face as she beamed up at me. There were the googly eyes I saw Nic and Cass giving each other earlier, except these were directed at me and I knew I was probably giving them right back.

Her attention broke, though, at the realization that it

was her turn and that we weren't the only two in the room; no matter how much it felt like it in that moment.

"I'm thankful to have found happiness again," she shared, her voice soft, but the emotion evident. Cass and Brian may not understand, but her friends and I knew how much that statement meant to her. "Never thought I would find it all the way in Scotland, but I'm thankful I took the opportunity to come here."

I managed to sneak a kiss to her cheek before Nic was enveloping her in a hug, causing her to momentarily let go of me. Sofia was joining them within seconds and placing a kiss to the top of both of their heads.

"We're so proud of you, mon cheri," Nic cooed.

There was a hint of tears building in the rim of Lydia's eyes as she looked to her friends with a shaky smile.

"Love you guys."

As soon as they let go of her and Sofia returned to her seat, Lydia ducked back into my side, hiding her face. I just gave her leg an encouraging squeeze, not wanting to draw more attention to her. After having seen her at a very low point, it was nice to hear and see that she was doing much better. To think I played at least a small part in that made me feel pretty pleased as well.

Chapter 18

Lydia

I stayed close to Alec's side, trying to get as much warmth from his body as possible as we walked through the snow-dusted streets of Edinburgh. Despite having on gloves, he had taken my right hand and tucked it into his coat pocket with his own wrapped tightly around it. My other hand was tucked into the crook of his arm which was almost just as warm.

Christmas lights hung on buildings, some draping across the street with festive designs like wreaths and snowflakes, giving the area a warm glow. It felt like something straight out of a Hallmark movie, but honestly that wasn't too far off to how life had felt with Alec in general lately.

"Just another block and then we'll be at the Christmas market and can get ye a hot chocolate," he promised.

I had admittedly been a little tentative to agree to visiting the outdoor Christmas market given the recent weather, but Alec had insisted that it wasn't something I should miss. Nic and Cass had visited earlier in the week and agreed wholeheartedly with him. So with the promise of several hot chocolates, as many as my heart desired, I agreed.

A little Christmas shopping for family and friends wouldn't be so bad either. I'd already built up quite the stock of souvenirs for my parents when they visited next week. I wouldn't mind getting another small gift or two for my friends and I had asked Alec to help me find something for Grandad. I'd spent a couple more nights playing board games with him while Alec was at his shows, the tourist season having picked up with the upcoming holidays, and quite enjoyed spending my afternoons in the cozy cottage. Much better than being alone in my flat.

My eyes widened as we finally rounded the last corner to the market. As expected, there was a long row of small booths resembling cottages lining either side of the road. What I hadn't expected was the fair rides behind the booths, shining just as bright as everything else with Edinburgh Castle lit up on the hill above it all.

"Wow," was all I could manage at first, earning a pleased grin from Alec.

"Come on. Let's get our drinks to warm us up while we shop at the booths. Then we can go on some of the rides if ye'd like."

I just grinned at him. "I'd love to!"

I was admittedly quite the amusement park fan.

However, I had never seen a winter fair before, let alone attended one. Back home in Missouri, all the theme parks closed for the winter or at least shut down their rides when the temperatures dropped low enough. The idea of the cold wind in my face as we whipped around sent a chill down my spine, but it was just more of an excuse to cuddle up to Alec.

Of course, it wasn't just your regular hot chocolate stand. There was an array of specialty hot chocolates and it was difficult to decide. I finally settled on the s'more one which included toasted marshmallow syrup, whip cream sprinkled with graham cracker crumbs, and a jumbo marshmallow torched to golden perfection to top it off. Alec had gone along a similar route with a cookie butter flavor that used white chocolate and included caramel drizzle, cinnamon, and a cookie balanced in the whip cream.

"I have to get a picture of these," I giggled once we were handed the drinks in their festive cups.

I took a step back as I dug my phone out of my pocket, careful not to spill my hot chocolate as I held it out in front of me so that Alec was visible behind it with his own cup.

"Smile!" I called out, grinning myself when he gave a cheesy smile over the top of his whip cream. Then he pretended to take a dramatic bite out of his cookie and I snapped that, too. "You are ridiculous."

"Ye say that, but I know that with you, that's a term of endearment," he smiled crookedly at me, a dark brow rising teasingly.

Not validating his response or denying it, I simply fell into step beside him and started walking again once I'd safely gotten my phone back in my pocket. Now I cupped my drink in both hands, relishing in the warmth emanating through my gloves. I figured it was safe enough to nibble on the marshmallow. While it wasn't the most graceful to just lift the cup up to my mouth and bite into it, plucking it from the whip cream would just make a sticky mess on my gloved fingers. This, of course, resulted in my nose dipping into the whip cream. My luck.

"Mm!" I mumbled around the sticky bite I'd taken. "Help?"

Alec looked down at me, his attention drawn from his own drink, and just chuckled when he saw me.

"Hold on. I got ye, hen."

He swiftly discarded one of his gloves and securely tucked it into his pocket before swiping his finger across the tip of my nose. His finger was surprisingly warm, but maybe that was just in contrast to the cool cream. He tilted his head to make sure he got it all before popping the finger into his mouth.

"Do we need to sit so ye can properly drink your chocolate?" he asked, a teasing tone in his voice.

No matter how much I wanted to protest, if only to save face, I knew that it was probably a much safer idea. I didn't need any more of this ending up on me, or worse, someone else.

"That may be best," I sighed.

Alec took a moment to look around before spotting some picnic tables and placing his hand on the small of my back to carefully guide me through the crowd to them. I was admittedly relieved to sit down and be able to place the drink on the table.

"Think it's cool enough?" I wondered.

I was glad he'd chosen to sit next to me instead of across the table, his shoulder pressed to mine. Without answering, he took a careful sip of his and then licked the cream left behind on his upper lip. So I wasn't the only messy one. That made me feel better.

"I'd say it's just about perfect. Maybe a little warm, but it feels good settling in your chest."

I at least finished off my marshmallow, deciding to suffer the cold for the moment and remove my glove to do so. But it was right back on as soon as I'd licked my fingers clean. Alec had been right; it was just cool enough that it didn't burn your tastebuds, but you still felt the warmth of it spread throughout your body. Just what I needed.

And the flavor? It was absolutely divine! S'mores alone were delicious, but this was even better (and somewhat less messier). The toasted marshmallow flavoring added just that little bit of extra sweetness to it.

"What do ye think?" Alec asked.

A glance at his cup showed that he was already halfway done. I, on the other hand, was savoring the drink.

"Best hot chocolate I've had by far. How is yours?"

He offered his mug to me. "Very sweet, but it reminds me of making Christmas cookies with Grannie and eating them straight out of the oven. When they're all warm and melt in your mouth."

I took a small sip. "You weren't kidding about the sweetness."

Fair is fair, so I slid my own drink over to him and sat back to wait for his opinion, rubbing my warm hands over my thighs under the table. His eyes widened a little and I smiled at the reaction.

"Tastes like you melted down a s'more. That is good!"

We finished off our drinks and watched people mill about the market. Everyone was in high spirits, enjoying the festivities and holiday season. I was excited that my parents would be here soon to join in. I was even more excited for them to meet the little family I'd created here. Nic and Sofia had popped in on several Facetime calls with my parents, so they were familiar with each other. I'd wanted them to meet Alec in person, though, and had only sent pictures of us and told stories to tide my mother over.

It wasn't working very well, but she had only one more week to suffer through.

"Do you have any ideas of what I could get Grandad?" I asked, leaning more into Alec once I finished my drink.

I was pleasantly cozy now with my tummy full of hot chocolate. Alec didn't seem inclined to move at the moment either, glancing around from our spot at some of the surrounding booths.

"I'd say a bookmark, but that man is a heathen and dog-ears his books no matter how many times I've insisted he shouldn't."

The absolute passion with which he said this, just made me smile. "What would you say if I told you that I just use random cards or scraps of paper for my bookmarks?" I asked curiously.

He simply shrugged the shoulder I wasn't leaning on and made a small, gruff noise in the back of his throat. "At least ye don't damage the book that way."

My smile only grew, but then I was looking around as well, lips pursed as I tried to think of something for the older Morgan.

"Does he mark in his books as well?"

"Thankfully, no. He's actually more organized in that sense and has notebooks he's filled with his thoughts on various books."

"Maybe a new pen and journal, then?"

"Aye," Alec nodded with a smile. "I think he'd like that very much. Especially coming from you."

We stood then and Alec grabbed our empty cups to throw away. I waited for him to rejoin me before slipping my hand into his and stepping back into the stream of fair-goers. We kept our eyes peeled, stopping at a few booths every now and then. I managed to find a few trinkets for my friends; an adorable highland cow ornament for Sofia and a beautifully intricate teacup for Nicolette.

It was Alec who spotted the booth which held a variety of leather-bound books and journals. Some were embossed with designs and I wandered closer to those, trying to see if a design stuck out to me.

Just then, the vendor stepped up next to us. "I can also emboss initials on them, if ye'd like. It only takes a few minutes."

I liked the simplicity of that instead of making a guess at a design.

"That would be wonderful," I smiled appreciatively. I gently tugged on Alec's hand as I stepped over to the other wall. "What color would he like?"

Alec didn't even hesitate, reaching for a dark, blue-green book and pulling it down. "This one." An emotion crossed his face that I couldn't quite place.

I merely nodded and took it from him, turning to the

vendor who was already readying his press. "Aye, a bonnie color ye picked here. What shall the initials be?"

"FAWM. Fergus Archibald William Morgan," Alec recited.

I waited until the vendor had set to work before I turned my attention to Alec, once again nestling my hands in the crook of his arm.

"So your brother was named after Grandad?"

"Aye. Though Archie would strangle anyone that called him Archibald," he chuckled before melodramatically rubbing at his own neck. "Believe me. I've made the mistake several times."

"Well that's what brothers are for, isn't it?"

The vendor took little time at all, but I couldn't stop from gushing over the beautiful script. Despite being separate tiles, the letters flowed together in a way that made it look handwritten.

"Oh, this is stunning. Thank you so much."

He wrapped the book in brown paper and then handed it to me along with a card. I was very much tempted to get a journal for myself. Maybe after my next paycheck. This last one had taken quite the blow with all the Christmas shopping.

I gingerly placed the parcel in my bag with the other gifts and then paid before following Alec further down the street. I assumed that our next destination was the fair rides now that our drinks had time to settle in our stomachs.

"What made you pick the blue-green color?" I asked, peeking curiously up at Alec.

In the warm lighting from the booths, I could just make out a slight blush on his cheeks.

"It's Grandad's favorite color. Well...ever since he met Grannie that is. It was the color of her eyes."

If the hot chocolate hadn't melted my heart with its heat, it was surely melted now.

"They had that rare kind of love, didn't they?" I asked gently.

Alec smiled a little, but nodded. "Aye. They did. One for the books."

"Have either of you ever thought of writing their story?"

His brows crinkled then.

"I dinna ken if he has. I mean, I ken plenty of stories from the two of them telling me over the years and of course witnessing their love firsthand." His lips pressed together and he let out a small hum. "May be an idea, though."

I smiled, "May be a great way to write down his memories of them."

Before they're completely gone, the little voice in my head added. I didn't dare voice that out loud, but when I looked at Alec, I could see the thought had crossed his mind, too; a slight downturn in the corner of his mouth.

"I could start writing some down when I visit with him. It would be a hell of a lot more enjoyable than having him destroy me in Scrabble every time."

That at least made him laugh. "Aye. I cannae blame ye there. You're a brave lass."

The colorful fair rides now stood above the final booths on the row, screams and laughter floating through the air. Most of them were familiar enough even if the names were different. The most notable, being a giant spinning swing that towered much higher than any fair ride I'd ever seen.

"What on earth is that?" I asked, head tilted completely back in order to look up at it.

Alec followed my gaze. "Ah, that's the Star Flyer. Think you're brave enough for it?"

That earned him a look, my brows coming together and down over my eyes. "Oh, Alec...darling. You don't know this yet, but I am an adrenaline junkie."

He just grinned back at me before giving my hand a tug. "Let's go then."

He guided me through the crowd to the ticket booth where he bought us each wristbands to ride as much as we wanted. This man clearly now knew the way to my heart. As soon as our wristbands were secured, we were off to join the line for the Star Flyer. It was clearly appropriately named, for the people now spinning at the peak of the pole looked about the size of the stars above them.

"An adrenaline junkie, eh?" Alec smirked down at me.

We stood close together, so I had no choice but to tilt my head back a ridiculous amount in order to be able to look at him.

"Yes, but not like a bungee jump off a bridge headfirst kind of adrenaline junkie. Like I enjoy wild roller-coasters and ziplining," I defended myself. "My parents and I had season passes to a theme park in Missouri when I was little and my dad and I would ride everything over and over. I love it."

"Well we'll see how ye do seventy meters in the air."

I shook my head. "I have no idea what seventy meters is, but I'll agree that this ride is very very tall."

Alec laughed as he wrapped an arm around my shoulders and pulled me securely into his chest so he could place a kiss to my forehead.

"My wee American. With your incorrect measurements."

Now that earned him a little nudge in the ribs, though I'm sure he hardly felt it through his thick sweater and coat. If anything, it just made him chuckle even more.

Thankfully, it was soon our turn and I was able to escape further teasing about American culture and how it was apparently wrong. Not that I one hundred percent disagreed with that; I clearly left the country for a reason.

The plastic seat was cold and I shivered a little as I slid back enough that we could properly buckle in. Like most swings, it was a simple buckle and then a metal bar that lowered down the chains until it settled over your lap. As soon as he was situated, Alec's arm was draped around my shoulders.

"Hopefully it's not too chilly up there for ye, hen."

I glanced up at the top of the pole where we would soon be spinning through the crisp air and then looked back at Alec.

"That just means we'll have to get another delicious hot chocolate," I shrugged with a grin.

He chuckled and nodded. "I think we can definitely manage that."

With everyone settled and their buckles checked, the swings started to move, slowly at first and then gaining speed as we rose higher. The force of it caused me to lean even more into Alec as he was in the outside seat.

Suddenly I heard a small sputtering sound and couldn't help but giggle when I turned to find him brushing strands of my hair out of his face.

"I'm so sorry!" Not that I could help it; the wind was whipping my already wild hair around and I had to reach up to tug my beanie further down.

"I like your hair, but I canna say I like it in my mouth,"

he laughed as well.

I did my best to gather the stray locks in my fist and tried to tuck it into the collar of my coat. Attempting to contain it within my hood was an impossible idea as I'd have to hold it tight to even keep it up on my head, so this was the next best thing.

The view quickly distracted me once we reached the very top. All the people below looked like little ants milling about the market, snagging those last minute gifts and decorations. The whole street glowed a warm yellow from the booths and the castle looked down at it all from its perch on the hill. Edinburgh had always been beautiful, but tonight it felt extra magical.

As one did when floating through the air, I happily kicked my feet back and forth, relishing in the feel of flying, even if it was cold. By the time we got back to the bottom and had slowed to a stop, I couldn't feel the tip of my nose. My legs were chilled even through my pants and I was a little stiff getting out of the seat.

Once we had stepped through the exit gate, Alec found a spot to stop to the side and turned to face me, his hands resting on my shoulders.

"Oh, hen," he chuckled, reaching up to cup my face in his somehow warm hands. "Your nose looks like a wee cherry, all red."

Before I could even respond, he was bending down to

place a kiss to my cold nose. Despite the chill, I was able to feel it and it absolutely melted me into a gooey puddle inside. Who needed hot chocolate to warm you up when you had the most adorable and doting boyfriend? I knew I had the goofiest smile on my face and it was only confirmed when I saw the pleased grin on Alec's own lips.

"What's that look for?"

"You're just insanely adorable and I can't handle it."

I couldn't tell if he was blushing or if his cheeks were just pink from the cold wind nipping at them on the swing, but I liked to think that I could make him just as flustered as he did me.

"Well, I can't handle how adorable ye are, either, so at least it's fair," he decided.

Again, those words wanted to bubble up my throat and into the cold night air, but then my heart squeezed at the idea that the sentiment may not be returned. Finding someone adorable and being in love with them were two completely different things. Thankfully, we were interrupted by the screams of the next round of riders for the Star Flyer, drawing both of our attention up as they ascended to the top.

Alec's hands fell back to my upper arms and he rubbed them gently. "Shall we get ye a hot chocolate now or do ye want to go on more rides?"

"More rides," I chose quickly with an excited grin. "We

can save the hot chocolate for the walk back to the car."

"As ye wish."

Chapter 19

Lydia

Alec had driven me to the airport to pick up my parents, but he decided to wait in the car for us, allowing me to have my reunion with them before automatically introducing them to the boyfriend. While I couldn't wait for them to meet, I was grateful for the opportunity to avoid Alec seeing me absolutely bawl my eyes out at the sight of my parents after so many months away from them.

My parents are fairly short, so I had to do a lot of peeking around other travelers in order to finally spot them. My mom saw me right away and instantly started running, suitcase trailing behind her while my dad struggled for a moment or two to figure out what was going on.

There's all those sayings like "distance makes the heart grow fonder" and "you don't know what you have until it's gone". I'd like to add that you don't know what you have until it's back. The second my mom wrapped me up in her arms and her familiar scent, I was hit hard with how much I had missed her. Between adjusting to Scotland, my new job, and my relationship with Alec, I had enough distractions that I didn't often dwell on what I had left behind in Missouri.

My father wrapped both of us up in his arms when he finally caught up and I felt him place a kiss to my head. I could've sworn I even heard him sniffle a little. We probably looked insane, being as emotional as we were, but surely we weren't the only ones.

Finally they pulled back and within seconds my mom's hands were cupping my cheeks as she looked me over, eyes teary like my own. She didn't say anything for a good while, just taking me in.

"Oh, honey. I've missed you so much."

I smiled shakily, "I've missed you guys, too. I can't wait to show you around."

"And show us this handsome boyfriend of yours?" she raised her brows with a small smirk that made me blush. Especially in front of my father.

"He's out in the car now. He wanted to give us space and then we thought we'd all go get lunch together."

"Sounds great! I could definitely eat," my dad patted his stomach which made me laugh and my mom roll her eyes.

"The meal on the airplane was actually pretty good."

"I'm glad. And I'm just so glad you're here." I gave them each one more hug before we headed out to the parking lot to find Alec.

Wanting him to have a heads up, I texted to let him know we were coming. When we arrived, he was leaning against the back of his car, the trunk already open for my parents' luggage. My mom gave my arm a squeeze at the sight of him, leaning over to whisper in my ear.

"He's even more handsome in person. And so tall!"

My cheeks flushed, but I couldn't hide my smile as I took him in. He looked extra handsome today in his dark jeans and button up. He had wanted to look nice for my parents.

"Mom, Dad. This is Alec," I gestured towards him.

"Hello, Mr. and Mrs. Foster," he greeted before holding out his hands. "Here. I'll take your bags for ye."

My dad didn't hesitate at all to roll his closer, clearly tired of lugging the thing around. "Thank you, son."

He then nudged my mom's luggage over as well and Alec deftly lifted them into the trunk, before closing it and turning to smile warmly at my parents.

"I take it a nice meal wouldna come amiss for ye. Lydia and I thought we'd take ye to the pub by her flat."

"Oh, I could eat anything at the moment," my mom laughed self-deprecatingly.

My dad couldn't help but add on, "And I wouldn't mind a nice beer along with it."

Alec just took it all in stride. "Aye, well there will be

plenty of quality beers there as well, sir. I can promise ye that."

He moved to open the back door for my mother who smiled widely at the gesture and thanked him before slipping in. Then it was my door he was opening. Our eyes met and I just beamed at him, stroking a hand momentarily down his upper arm; a subtle, but intimate gesture letting him know he was doing great. He just smiled back and waited for me to settle in before shutting the door and moving around to the driver's seat.

The drive through Edinburgh mostly consisted of him playing tour guide and sharing history about the city and different buildings we passed. My dad absolutely ate it up, asking clarifying questions and whole-heartedley ogling out the window at everything. He'd always been interested in history and, due to his heritage, had a specific soft spot for the UK.

"I can see why you like it so much, Lydia. This city is absolutely beautiful," my mom finally managed to chip in.

"Isn't it?" I grinned.

Alec

I was absolutely sweating and I thanked myself for having the foresight to wear all dark colors so hopefully Lydia's parents wouldn't notice the pit stains. For all I knew, they were judging my driving skills as we wound through the city traffic, so I had done my best to distract them with facts and short little history lessons. It seemed to be working for the most part, at least with her father.

Lydia was the first to hop out once I turned off the car, happily leading her parents into the pub as I followed behind. I made sure to step around them, though, to open the door, smiling politely as they all thanked me. But Lydia got an extra special smile.

We managed to find a booth and I slid in next to her, feeling a good deal easier now that she was close enough I could touch her. I settled for pressing my knee against hers.

"Now I ken Guinness is an Irish beer and ye probably ken what it tastes like already, but I promise ye it tastes so much fresher over here than it does for ye across the pond."

"I will never turn down a Guinness and the fresher the better," her father smiled widely at me.

As if summoned by the name of the infamous beer, our

waitress appeared to get us started with drinks while we continued to look over the menu. Even that didn't take terribly long. I believe Lydia's parents were just happy to be eating something that wasn't served on an airplane and more interested in catching up.

"I've got everything planned for while you guys are here," Lydia sat up excitedly. "We've got a tour of the castle tomorrow and then one night we have to go to the Christmas market that Alec took me to. Mom, you'll love all the shops and they have fair rides we can go on, Dad."

She shared the other plans and ideas she'd come up with to make the most of their short time here. My stomach did a little flip at the mention of Christmas with my own family. Not only had I just met her parents, but this would be Lydia's first time meeting my family as they hadn't been able to visit me and Grandad since we'd started dating. It would be an eventful holiday for sure.

"Thank you, Alec, for inviting us to celebrate with your family. I really hope we aren't intruding," her mother fussed.

"Not at all," I assured her. "My family will be more than happy to have ye."

My mum had been over the moon actually when I'd suggested the idea. The more the merrier had always been her slogan when it came to get-togethers and celebrations.

"I hope ye don't mind three wee bairns running

around, though."

"Bairns?" Mr. Foster asked, his pint paused halfway to his lips and his bushy eyebrows pulling together slightly.

"Oh. My nieces," I explained quickly.

Lydia was also quick to chime in, "They call little kids and babies, bairns. Usually I hear Alec call them 'wee heathens'."

She smirked over at me then and I smirked back at her attempt at my accent. I couldn't deny it, though. The three of them were quite the handful.

"I love little ones!" Lydia's mother cooed, eyes wide in excitement. "I wish I would have known. I would have brought them something."

"Believe me, they have more than they could ever need."

"Lydia. Remind me to find something for Alec's parents at the Christmas market to thank them for hosting us." Her eyes turned back to me again and I could see that they were almost the exact same color as Lydia's. "You'll help me pick something they like, won't you?"

"Of course," I nodded amiably.

Our food arrived shortly and conversation slowed slightly as everyone dug into their meals. For lunch portions, they were still quite hearty meals which seemed more than okay with her parents.

Lydia had mostly cleared her plate when she placed her

hand on my leg, "I'm going to run to the restroom real quick." Her eyes zoned in on her parents accusingly. "Be nice while I'm gone."

Her father just scoffed at the assumption that they would be anything but kind and I sent her a reassuring smile that I'd be fine. I didn't figure their attitude toward me would change drastically once she was away and I had been correct. Mrs. Foster looked at me, a gentle smile on her lips, but a serious look in her eyes.

"I'm only saying this now, because I might embarrass or upset Lydia if I said it in front of her, but...thank you. It's been too long since we've seen our daughter so happy."

Right away, I felt the heat creeping up my neck, threatening a blush, so I ducked my head and shook it dismissively. "Och. It's all her," I protested.

Mr. Foster shook his head. "You didn't know her the last few years. She looks and acts more like herself now that she's been here in Scotland and we appreciate how much you've looked after her and cared for her."

"She makes it easy," was all I could say.

Lydia had been honest with me about how much her job in Missouri had taken a toll on her mental health and the extent of her depression. I knew I'd only seen the tiniest glimpse of it that one time. It was hard to see such a loving and radiant person reduced to a shadow of themselves. I could only imagine the pain her parents had gone through the last few years watching her and the relief they now felt at seeing her more closely resemble the daughter they knew and loved so dearly.

"It's hard having her so far away, but knowing that she's back to her happy self and has you makes it more bearable."

I knew my cheeks were full-on pink now, no matter how much I tried to hide it. So I just met each of their gazes in turn so they knew how honest I was being.

"It's my pleasure."

Chapter 20

Alec

The presents had been exchanged and my nieces had already opened several of their new toys, the remnants of their packages scattered about the living room. Now everyone was enjoying cookies, hot tea, and each other's company. Currently, I was caught up in conversation with my brother, Archie, but I kept glancing over at Lydia again and again.

She was sat cross-legged by the tree with my youngest niece tucked comfortably in her lap as they read the new book she'd received from Grandad. The oldest two stood behind Lydia, braiding her long hair. Or at least attempting to. Mostly it looked like a bunch of twists, but Lydia didn't seem to mind. I couldn't help but smile at the sight, a warm feeling in my chest.

My family absolutely adored her and she'd of course hit it off right away with my sister-in-law. The same could be said for her parents. Her mother and mine had been chatting the entire time and Grandad was now giving her father an intense lecture that he seemed completely enraptured by. The blending of families for a major holiday honestly couldn't have gone more perfectly.

"She's so wonderful with the girls," my sister-in-law, Darcy, commented as she sat down on Archie's other side. "I don't think Eliza has ever sat so still to read a book."

"Liza has never sat so still for anything," Archie chuckled. "We may be asking Lydia to babysit."

"Now don't go stealing my girlfriend from me," I teased.

Darcy waved her hand dismissively. "Oh, ye know the girls would love their Uncle Alec to come as well. May be best to have the two of ye teamed up against them. Especially come bedtime."

My gaze went back to Lydia and as if she felt it, she looked up from the book and sent me the most breathtaking smile. I knew it; I was madly, head over heels in love with her. But with that wonderful feeling came the heartbreak of knowing she would be leaving soon. Her time here in Scotland was already halfway up and then what? It's not as though I could leave and follow her to America. While my work easily allowed for that, there was no way I could leave Grandad. Things would only get worse with him from here and I had promised myself and my family that I would support him through it.

But, God. To lose my Lydia, my sunshine. The prospect of those coming months without her seemed bleak and gray, especially knowing that I'd be slowly losing my other favorite person in the entire world. The thought of it was all too much and I had to fight to swallow against the lump in my throat.

"I um..." Slight panic was settling into my chest and my flight instinct was kicking in. "I'm going to get some more tea."

I hoped that neither of them noticed that my cup was still halfway full as I hastily stood and made my way to the kitchen. Barely managing to set my cup on the counter without spilling it, I braced my hands against the cool top and closed my eyes, forcing myself to take deep breaths.

The worsening of Grandad's disease was inevitable. It did nothing to worry about it. I needed to embrace the time I had with him and soak up every moment; not be panicking in the kitchen on Christmas. Probably his last Christmas where he was mostly himself.

Before my mind could spiral anymore, I hastily poured more tea into my cup, almost spilling it over the edge, and then stirred a good helping of sugar. It did little to distract my thoughts, but it at least kept my hands moving.

"There you are."

I spun around as if I'd been caught with my hand in the cookie jar by my mother and then relaxed when I saw Lydia and heard her laugh.

"Sorry. I didn't mean to scare you. Lord knows what my

hair looks like."

Braids and twists were everywhere and one in particular hung almost directly down the middle of her face.

"Well if they were going for a Medusa look, they nailed it," I replied as seriously as possible.

Lydia's jaw dropped, but I saw the grin on her lips which just made me smile. The tightness in my chest eased.

"Dinna give me that look. Medusa was a beautiful woman. So beautiful she caught the eye of Poseidon," I tried to save myself.

She shook her head, "Don't finish that story. Stop while you're ahead."

She wasn't wrong. In that version of her story, Poseidon had taken advantage of her in Athena's temple which led to the curse of snakes for hair and the ability to turn anyone to stone who met her gaze.

Like magnets, we stepped closer to each other and when she was within reach, I moved the braid back so I could see her face properly. Then I leaned down to place a kiss to her lips, pleased whenever she returned it and stepped even closer.

"Can I give you your present now?" she asked once she pulled away, a hopeful smile on her face.

"Only if I can give ye yours."

"Deal," she nodded, causing the braid to fall back into her face.

I bit my lip to stifle a laugh, but then she was giggling and I couldn't help myself. I reached up for the braid and began to undo it, carefully unwinding the auburn strands.

"Annabeth is going to be so upset with you. She worked hard on that one," she playfully scolded.

"She won't even notice."

Lydia shrugged, "When she does, I'm blaming you."

"Och. I can handle Annabeth. I'll just toss her over my shoulder and tickle her 'til she forgets."

Braid now gone, I tucked the hair behind her ear and eyed the others. They weren't as obtrusive as the one I had just removed, mostly tucked within her wild locks. It gave almost a viking woman look to her.

"Your gift is up in my room if ye'd like to exchange gifts there. Not have everyone ogling us."

"That was exactly my thoughts. Yours is under my coat. I'll grab it and meet you up there?" she raised her brows in question.

I nodded and stole one more kiss before turning to clean up my small mess from the tea. I'd come back for it later, though it'd definitely be cold by then.

Not wanting to walk through the chaos of the living room, I cut through the library and up the stairs. Lydia's present sat on my nightstand, a small box wrapped in blue

paper with a silver bow. I picked it up and then sat down at
the edge of my bed, just in time for her to step through the
door, her hands behind her back. They stayed there even as
she came to join me, the package kept securely out of sight.
I just eyed her suspiciously.

"What? I don't want you to guess what it is," she
explained.

"Okay, so am I giving ye your gift first, then?"

She bit her lip as she thought it over before finally
nodding. She must have set my present on the mattress
behind her, because her hands moved in front of her, but I
didn't even see a glimpse of the gift. Ignoring it for now, I
held out the small box to her, prepared to explain it when
she opened it.

She was careful in her unwrapping, sliding the ribbon
off and setting it to the side before she ripped the paper.
When she opened the box, she gasped softly at the silver
hair slide balanced on a pad of velvet. Her finger carefully
traced the intricate pattern of the Celtic knot.

"It's for your hair. I know you're always trying to get it
out of your face and I thought ye could use this to pin it
back." Now it was my turn to trace the knot, finger lightly
brushing against hers. "It's a Celtic knot and the pin is a
Scottish thistle."

So ye can remember Scotland when ye go back. I bit
back the words, not wanting to spoil the moment with my

fretting. They were all forgotten, though, when those green eyes met mine, a certain sparkle in them.

"I love it, Alec. It's absolutely beautiful." She picked up the slide to examine it further. "Will you put it in for me?"

I laughed unexpectedly. "Well, I'll try."

I took the slide as she turned so her back was to me and removed the pin, carefully setting it to the side for now. Thankfully, she was already pulling half of her hair back, clearly knowing where she liked her hair to be split. I waited and then held the silver knot in place while gently pushing the pin through one side, under her hair, and back through the other.

At the drop of my hands, she turned more to the side. "What do ye think?"

"Stunning, hen," I confessed. "And ye look like a proper Celt with the braids and the knot."

She smiled at that and then reached to her side, returning with my gift. It was wrapped in floral Christmas paper that Lydia had used with all of her gifts.

"Okay. Your turn now."

I smiled at her as I took the gift and then carefully unwrapped it. From the moment I saw the corner, I knew exactly what it was. The leather journal very much resembled the one she'd bought Grandad except for a few details. Instead of my initials in the corner, 'A & L' was embossed in the center of the cover. The cover which just happened to be a green that reminded me very much of the Scottish hills and thus, Lydia's own eyes. Had she done that on purpose?

Her eyes were locked on the book, clearly avoiding my own, and there was a pink flush to the apple of her cheeks.

"I um...I've already started to write in it, but please don't read it until I leave. I'd die of embarrassment if you read it in front of me."

That just made me even more curious. But I set the journal to the side and cupped her chin, tilting her head up so I could see those lovely green eyes of hers.

"I love it, hen. It's beautiful and I can't wait to read what you've written."

I didn't even give her a chance to respond as I leaned in for another kiss, this one lingering much longer as we both poured our love into it. Or it was at least definitely love on my end. I could only hope the sentiment was returned.

Lydia and her parents were the first to leave, soon followed by Archie and Darcy who each carried a sleeping daughter and held the hand of the eldest, Julianna, who looked as if she was about to fall asleep standing up. My parents were staying in the other spare room, but they were enjoying another cup of tea with Grandad. I kissed them all goodnight and then retired to my bedroom. I wasn't tired, but I was eager to see what Lydia had written in the journal.

When I opened the cover, a small piece of paper fell out. I unfolded it to read the short message.

I thought our story might be interesting to write as well. Of course, I don't expect you to write Grandad's stories and ours by yourself, so I already started us off.

Sure enough, on the very first page was Lydia's tidy handwriting with a date at the top of the entry that must've been the night we first met.

August 17th

I attended the "Spirit of Scotland" show with Sofia, Nic, and some of our coworkers to get a taste of Scottish culture. As the entree was served, our host gave some history of Scotland and the origins of its music and dancing. The two girls who had greeted us came on stage, accompanied by two other girls and a few men. The men were definitely what had the attention of my colleagues and I noticed Nicolette giggling; most likely remembering the conversation from the bus about the Scottish men and their kilts. Or rather what

may or may not be underneath.

I'd be lying, though, if I said the men didn't have my attention

as well. Or rather one in particular. He was broader than the

others with curly, dark hair and dark stubble to match. He could

give Outlander's Sam Hueghan a run for his money, but then

again I'd always preferred darker haired men.

I couldn't help but smile to myself at the comparison, knowing Lydia's fondness for the show. I was intrigued to read more, wanting to know her side of events as I was more than familiar with my own. So, I left the journal face down on the pillow next to mine as I readied for bed and then slipped under the blankets to settle in and read the rest of what she'd written.

Chapter 21

Lydia

I turned this way and that, checking over my reflection in the mirror and assuring myself that I had in fact put the hair slide in correctly. It was fairly tricky to figure out, what with the knot creating all sorts of holes for me to incorrectly stick the pin through, but I was determined to figure it out myself instead of enlisting Sofia or Nic's help.

A glance at the clock next to my bed showed that I was about right on time for when Alec said he would be by to pick me up. I made sure I had everything I needed in my purse and took my heeled boots with me to the living room to slip on. Getting fleece-lined tights had been one of the best purchases I'd made, allowing me to wear dresses in the cold Scottish winter. They were honestly warmer than my jeans or any other pants I owned.

I waited to put on my coat until I got the text that he was here, not wanting to sweat in my cozy flat. In typical 'millennial' fashion, I ended up scrolling through social media as I waited for the text, catching up on loved ones back home. Honestly, I lost track of time between sending likes and leaving comments. When I looked at the top of my screen for the time, I was shocked to see that it was a good twenty minutes past the time Alec had said.

He could've been late for any number of reasons; the most likely one being that Orla had been running behind in getting there to stay with Grandad. I wasn't about to be the crazy girlfriend who texted him wondering where he was when he was most likely already on his way.

So I went back to my scrolling, watching videos now to keep myself entertained and sharing some with Sofia and Nicolette that I thought they'd appreciate. The type of videos I sent to each of them was vastly different, but some I sent in the group chat to both of them. Those were typically videos making fun of students and their crazy antics.

At some point, I kicked off my boots and tucked my feet up on the couch next to me. Now Alec was more than an hour and a half late. I sent a quick text to see if he was okay, tugging a blanket onto my lap. When twenty minutes went by without a response, I decided that this warranted me calling him whether he was possibly driving or not. The phone rang and rang before going to his voicemail.

In a last ditch effort, I sent a message to Orla, but got no response from her either. It was past eight o'clock at this point and even if I did get a response from Alec, I wasn't feeling up to going out anymore. Everything would be closing up anyways.

> Please call me when you can.
> I'm worried about you. x

With a sigh, I got up from the couch and headed to my bedroom to change into pajamas. I kept my phone within easy reach even as I moved between bedroom and bathroom to remove my makeup, just in case. It rang just as I was double checking that my door was locked and the living room lamp was off, Alec's name and a picture of us lighting up the screen. I was quick to snatch it up, barely registering hitting the answer button.

"Alec! Are you okay?"

There was no hiding the panic and concern in my voice.

"Lydia. I'm so sorry."

The regret was obvious in his own voice, but so was the utter exhaustion.

"Alec. Please tell me you and Grandad are okay," I begged. I knew that something with Grandad would be the only thing that would keep him from answering his phone. It terrified me to think of what it might be.

"We're okay now."

I sank down onto my bed with a breath, though I wasn't sure if it was from relief or concern that something had truly happened. Alec was silent for a moment on the other end, but I knew he was gathering his thoughts, processing the events of the night.

"I was just about to leave. Orla was here and he was reading. I'm not sure what he asked her, but then he was yelling so I hurried back to the library to help. He–" He paused, the lump in his throat audible when he began to talk again. "He didn't recognize me. He kept calling me my father's name and rambling on about how I had disappointed my mother. M–my grannie."

Even though I knew Grandad sometimes had episodes of aggression, I had never seen one and found it hard to picture such a kind man so angry. I couldn't imagine how that felt for Alec.

"I tried to calm him, to reason with him, but he wasna having it. I placed my hand on his shoulder to see if I could get him to sit down and then next thing I knew, I was lying on the floor with Orla fussing over me. He apparently knocked me good with the book he'd been reading."

I gasped, imagining it in my head. Grandad had to have hit him good if he passed out for at least a few seconds. What if Orla hadn't been there?

"Can I see you?"

He gave a pitiful attempt at a laugh. "I'm no so much to look at now. He gave me quite the shiner." He interrupted before I could argue with him, "But I'd like to see ye, hen.

Very much."

"I'll be there soon, okay?"

"Okay. Be safe and text me."

I agreed and then hung up, the desire to see him in person far stronger than the desire to stay on the line with him. Now was not a time to care about how I looked, so I slipped on a hoodie and a pair of joggers over my sleep shorts. Somehow I managed to put on shoes while also putting on my coat. I called for a cab as I caught the elevator down to the lobby and waited inside until I saw him pull up. All the while, I texted Alec to let him know I was on the way and again when we were close.

When we pulled up, I could see the silhouette of him standing in the doorway, backlit by the light from the library at the end of the short hall. I didn't even bother getting a good look at his face as I rushed into his arms, burying my own face into his chest and holding him tight. He wrapped me up just as tightly and I could feel his breath in my hair as he nuzzled the top of my head.

After a few moments, he pulled back, keeping his arms around me as he tugged me fully inside the house.

"Let's go sit by the fire. Ye'll freeze to death out here."

I wasn't about to argue with him when a nice fire and cuddles on the couch were calling my name. I followed him in and waited while he locked the door behind us before leading me to the library.

It wasn't until we were fully in the light that I was able to see his face, the skin around his left eye dark purple already and a spot of red on the outside corner where blood vessels had burst. I couldn't stop myself from reaching up to cup his cheek and tilt his head for a better view.

"Grandad never was one for light reading," he joked. "Never thought I'd get beaten up by Charles Dickens, though."

I leaned back and frowned up at him. How on earth was he joking about this?

"Not funny."

"Oh, come on, hen. It's a little funny," he tried that charming smile on me. "How many people can say they've gotten a black eye from *Great Expectations*?"

I just leveled him with a look, but that didn't damper his smile. That is until I lowered my hand and my fingers brushed just a little too close to his eye, causing him to wince. I gasped, instinctively taking a step back from him, and clutched my hands to my chest.

"I'm so sorry!"

He shook his head and reached out for my arm before I could move any further away.

"It's fine, hen. Just a little tender," he insisted. "How about we go sit on the couch? The ibuprofen hasn't fully kicked in yet and my head's still throbbing some."

I quickly obliged and moved to sit at one end of the couch. I was just about to look for a blanket when Alec gingerly laid down and rested his head in my lap. My hands hovered over him for a moment, not really sure what to do. I figured my safest bet was to let my one hand just rest on his chest, no harm done there, and the other instinctively fell to his dark curls. He didn't wince or even twitch, so I took that as a good sign and began to stroke my fingers through the strands. Alec let out a sigh and I felt his body relax under my touch.

The bruise was already bad for such a recent injury; I could only imagine what it would look like in the morning. Hopefully he didn't have any shows soon or if he did, one of the girls had enough makeup to help him cover it up.

As I sat there, I listened for any sign of Grandad, but there was nothing but the crackling fire. Orla must've been able to get him to bed. I wondered if he'd realized what happened or not before falling asleep. Either way, I knew he'd be heartbroken.

More often than not, it was easy to forget about the disease. The evenings I had spent with him, there'd been a few missing memories here and there when he'd told me stories, but not a full blown episode. Alec and Orla were much more familiar with those than I was. Sure, I'd heard of him getting upset or frustrated, but never aggressive and especially not towards Alec. But then of course, he apparently didn't realize that it was his beloved grandson. Had that happened before?

"Lydia?" Alec's voice broke me from my thoughts and I turned my gaze to his.

I'd stared so long at the fire that I could see the dancing flames reflected behind my eyelids when I blinked, so it took me a moment to focus on him.

"Will ye stay the night with me?"

His voice was quiet and much less confident than usual, making him almost sound like a little kid. My heart still did a flip flop in my chest. Apparently I didn't respond quick enough or my face portrayed something, because he sat up and turned on the couch to face me, brows pinched together.

"Ye dinna have to, I just—I'd like it if ye would stay."

It was late and I wouldn't feel as safe taking a cab home now, but I also wouldn't want Alec to have to get out in order to drive me home. And a big part of me yearned to stay with him and continue to comfort him. A prick of nerves made it hard to say yes right away, though.

"I want to, but..." How did I say it? More importantly, would he even understand? "Not that I think you'd make a move in your condition or with Grandad here, but...I'm asexual."

The wrinkle between his brows relaxed and I noticed the corner of his lip twitch, but I couldn't tell what that meant. I was currently taking every miniscule expression in, trying to determine if this was the end of us. He wouldn't be the first.

"Okay."

"Okay?"

He shrugged easily. "I dinna care, Lydia."

I just stared at him for a few moments, body still tensed as I tried to process his response. He reached out for me and took my hands in his, soothingly caressing the back of them with his thumbs.

"Hen...I haven't just been biding my time. And I hope I never gave ye a reason to think that or made ye feel pressured to be more physical than ye'd like."

I quickly shook my head then and suddenly gripped at his hands. "No. No. You never have. Any physical intimacy between us, I have wholeheartedly wanted," I insisted.

His body relaxed at the reassurance and I found mine relaxing as well. He used his hold on my hands to gently tug me closer and I obliged, moving until our legs were pressed together and he could wrap an arm around me. His dark eyes bore into mine for who knows how long, the fire's reflection almost making them golden.

"I love you, Lydia, and though you are as bonnie as can be, I love ye for much more than your looks. It's the warmth ye exude everywhere ye go. Ye make everyone feel seen and understood and I know that's why your students love ye so much. You're a safe place. For them and especially for me."

He bent his head down to gently rest his forehead against mine, our noses brushing against each other. I reached up with one of my hands to cup his neck and prayed he was too close to see the tears building up in my eyes.

"I love you, too, Alec," I whispered. "I'm absolutely head over heels."

I felt more than saw him smile, his lips brushing against my own as they curved up.

"Yeah?"

I laughed softly, happily. "Yeah."

Then his lips were pressed firmly to mine, both arms wrapping me up in his embrace and I draped my own around his neck to keep him close. It felt good to have it off my chest; both my sexuality and my feelings for Alec. God knows I'd kept the true extent of my feelings from him for long enough. It was exciting to know that he felt the same.

He let out a small groan suddenly and pulled back, his face scrunched up as he reached up to tenderly touch his nose.

"I think he got me in the nose, too," he grumbled.

I just shook my head. "Who would've thought Grandad had such a good arm on him?"

His eyes popped open and he looked at me in shock

before busting up laughing. I grinned and let out a giggle myself.

"Okay, so it is a little funny," I admitted.

"Glad ye finally admitted it," he smiled smugly. "But don't tell Hayden and Graham what happened. We'll say I was defending your honor and the other guy looks even worse."

Now it was my turn to drop my head back with a laugh. As if Alec would ever physically fight anyone; He was too sweet for that. But I nodded anyway and patted his shoulder.

"You got it."

He just grinned at me some more and snuck one more careful kiss before moving to stand, capturing one of my hands in his to pull me up.

"Come on. Let's go to bed."

He made sure to smother the fire and turn off all the lights before leading me upstairs. I was admittedly exhausted, more from the emotions of the evening than anything else. Yet there was still a buzz throughout me at our earlier confessions.

He paused at the top of the stairs and nodded towards his room. "I'll let ye have the bathroom first and I can get ye something to sleep in."

I laughed a little shyly. "Actually, I'm already in pajamas. I was getting ready for bed when you called, so I just threw on sweats over the top."

He smiled at that and I couldn't help but smile back, feeling quite comfortable despite my earlier reservations. Usually first sleepovers with my significant others had been awkward, but not with Alec. I knew he truly meant what he'd said and I felt safe with him.

"Well then, I'll find ye a toothbrush and then we can go to bed."

I followed him to the bathroom where he found a new toothbrush in the cabinet and then left to change himself. I made sure to take enough time with my nightly routine so he'd have the opportunity to fully dress before I returned. Not that it was necessary; He was already in the hall waiting on me.

"I'll be right in," he promised, now taking my place in the bathroom.

I tiptoed across the hall and began to discard my hoodie and joggers, folding them up and placing them on the trunk at the foot of his bed. I wasn't sure which side Alec preferred to sleep on, so I just sat on the trunk as I pulled my hair up into a messy bun on the top of my head. The last thing Alec needed was to be smothered by my hair in his sleep. In fact, maybe it would be best if I slept on his right side, away from his black eye and sore nose.

He answered my wonderings as soon as he walked in, shutting off the overhead light so there was only the bedside lamp on and then climbing in on the left side of the bed.

"Come 'ere, hen," he requested softly, waiting with the blankets turned back.

I didn't hesitate to move around to the other side of the bed and slip under the covers. The large quilt weighed comfortably on me as Alec practically tucked me in next to him. Again, I was surprised by my lack of reservation as I curled up at his side.

"Feel free to push me to the other side of the bed if you need to," I joked, watching him shut off the lamp.

"Och," he sighed as he settled back into the bed and draped an arm over me to tuck me even more securely against him. "I'd never push ye away."

I was glad the dark hid my giddy smile and blush.

Chapter 22

Alec

I instinctively woke whenever I heard Grandad's bedroom door open and his slippered feet shuffle down the hall. However, I was quickly distracted by the throbbing on the left side of my face, groaning a little. Clearly I was due for another dose of ibuprofen and an ice pack. Even more reason to get up and make sure he got his coffee and breakfast alright.

My groan caused Lydia to shift in the bed next to me, letting out a long sigh when she sunk back into the mattress, clearly still in a deep sleep. I couldn't help but smile despite the pain, slowly reaching over to brush a wayward strand from her face and tucking it behind her ear. The corner of her lip twitched.

I recalled what she'd shared with me last night and was even more pleased to find her still asleep beside me. It would've been easy for her to insist on going back to her flat and I would've one hundred percent understood. I'd meant what I said; Lydia meant more to me than simple sex. I desired and needed her in other ways; ways that apparently both of us thought were more important. I could go without sex if it meant having Lydia in my life. Easy.

My heart gave another squeeze and I was beaming so big it made my bruised cheek ache even more. She loved me. We'd both taken a leap of faith with our confessions last night and I hoped she was just as pleased with them as I was. Actually, I was quite over the moon about it if I was being honest. It'd been a good long time since I'd felt for someone the way I did for Lydia.

A clatter from downstairs drew my attention and I quickly, but carefully climbed out of the bed, doing my best not to disturb her. The wood floors were cold under my bare feet as I slipped out of the room and made my way downstairs to the kitchen where I could hear muttered curses.

"Where is that damn coffee?"

"Top shelf, Grandad. Next to the fridge," I directed.

He must've heard me coming, because he didn't even flinch, just grumbled once more under his breath about how I needed to stop moving things around on him. I didn't mention that the coffee beans had been in that exact spot ever since I'd moved in and simply stepped around him to get my own coffee mug out and one for Lydia as well. If anything, I'd take some tea up to her in my room. And possibly a pastry. That'd be cute.

"Oi!" Grandad gasped suddenly and I looked at him in confusion. "D'ye get in a fight last night? I didna think you and Lydia were going to such a place. Someone didna try to rob ye while ye were out, did they?"

I quickly shook my head to stop his spiraling thoughts and then winced as that just made the throbbing worse. Before I answered, I snatched the bottle of pain relievers from the cabinet and popped some into my mouth, swallowing them dry. Thankfully, Grandad waited without any further guesses as to the cause of my somewhat gruesome appearance.

"I had a disagreement, but not on my date." I paused, weighing the options of telling him exactly what happened. Ultimately, I decided it wasn't fair to keep it from him, no matter how much it might hurt the both of us. I looked him in the eyes, steeling myself for his reaction. "You and I got into it last night. Ye werena happy with Orla, so I stepped in and ended up getting *Great Expectations* to the face."

His eyes widened and I felt a tiny crack in my heart at the expression on his face. His weathered hand lifted to reach up and touch my cheek, but he stopped himself and forced it back down to his side. That might've hurt even worse.

"I did that to ye?" he asked, his voice hoarse.

"I kinda asked for it. We both know it's a fool who steps up to ye when you're upset," I tried to joke.

It didn't land. He was still looking at me with that soul-crushing look as if I'd just kicked his favorite puppy in front of him. I knew, because that's exactly how I felt, too.

I reached for his hand now and held it in both of mine, noting how fragile it felt even though I knew that hand had written hundreds of essays and novels and held stacks of books that would make tables groan under their weight.

"It's alright, Grandad. I ken ye didna mean to hurt me."

He shook his head as if in a haze. "I'd never hurt ye."

I gave him a small smile. "I know." I placed a kiss to his knuckles and then lowered his hand, giving it a pat. "Now ye can make it up to me by sharing a couple of your morning rolls Orla made ye with me and Lydia."

His bushy brows crinkled as he glanced around. "Lydia is here?"

"Aye, she came over last night and ended up staying."

His eyebrows shot up now, almost disappearing under his fringe of gray hair, and I scoffed.

"Och! Not like that! I was hurting and she stayed to comfort me."

Grandad just made a noise in the back of his throat that was somehow distinctly Scottish. I knew his meaning, but I wasn't going to explain myself any more. Besides, Lydia's sexuality was not mine to share, nor Grandad's to try and understand. If he could.

Either way, he retrieved several morning rolls from the

pantry and placed them in the oven for a few moments to warm while I worked on the coffee. As soon as I'd pressed the start button, I went to the freezer to find the ice pack Orla had given me last night when I'd first regained consciousness. While I didn't like having the cold against my skin when we were still in the midst of winter and a fire hadn't been started in the hearth yet, it provided enough relief that I could put up with the chill.

Grandad could be trusted with the coffee now that all he had to do was wait for it to finish brewing and pour it in his mug. So I got to work on filling the tea kettle as best I could with one hand and placing it on the stove to heat up for Lydia's tea.

"She drinks chamomile, doesn't she?" Grandad piped up next to me, opening the cabinet that held a variety of teas.

I nodded with a soft smile, "Aye, she does."

He found the box of chamomile and filled a tea infuser with the leaves before setting it in the extra mug so it'd be ready once the water had boiled.

"Thank you, Grandad."

He merely waved me off and then nudged me out of the way whenever the coffee beeped to let us know it was done. "I was the first down here, so I get the first pour," he teased.

I just rolled my eyes playfully, but moved to the side

anyway. It felt nice to be teasing each other again and I was sure that we would be able to move on from last night. I had obviously already forgiven him, the trick would just be getting Grandad to forgive himself.

He filled my mug as well and made my coffee exactly how I liked (which was also his preferred way) and then slid the mug closer to me. We were easily slipping back into our morning routine.

"You go sit with your coffee and ice and I'll prepare the rolls and her tea," he insisted, nodding towards the dining room table.

Normally I would argue, but filling the tea kettle had been hard enough with one eye and one available hand. So I simply thanked him and then plopped down in one of the chairs to wait, bracing my elbow on the table since my arm was already tired.

My good eye watched him move about the kitchen, carefully removing the morning rolls from the oven and splitting them in half to spread butter and honey over them which instantly melted. The smell alone was heavenly. I knew they'd taste even better.

Then the kettle started to whistle and he was pouring the boiling water into the tea cup for Lydia. By the time he was done with her tea, my coffee had just cooled off enough for me to comfortably drink it.

"Here ye are." Grandad set down the tray that Grannie

used to use when we were sick in bed on the table in front of me. Now Orla mostly used it to bring Grandad his meals if he wouldn't leave his chair in the library for it. Which was fairly often. It was difficult to pull him from his books and writing. "Usually I would include a flower for your grannie when I surprised her with breakfast in bed, but...with it being winter and what not..." he trailed off with a shrug.

I lowered the ice from my face so I could smile properly up at him. "Lydia will love it. Especially knowing that ye made it for her."

I could've sworn his cheeks turned a shade of pink, but he just hid his shy smile behind his mug as he took a sip of coffee and headed to the library, snatching the plate he'd made himself of morning rolls. He was about as smitten with Lydia as I was.

I stood to top off my mug and then placed it on the tray before carefully carrying it upstairs to Lydia. I took the stairs extra slow, not wanting to spill either of our drinks. She was awake when I toed the door open, sitting criss-cross on my bed with her hoodie and joggers on again as she redid her bun.

"Good morning," I smiled.

She grinned back at me in the most adorably sleepy way. She must not have been awake for very long.

"Morning."

I set the tray down on the bed and then sat down next to her. "Grandad made ye tea and even shared his morning rolls," I explained.

She giggled as she gently picked up her tea cup. "I'll have to thank him." She took a sip and then looked at me, a touch more serious now. "How is he?"

I took a bite of a roll to buy myself time to be able to respond without the lump in my throat being audible at the memory of the look on Grandad's face. I just didn't think about how hard it would be to swallow a mouthful of bread and honey around that lump. There was no choice but to take a big gulp of coffee no matter how warm it was. Then I cleared my throat and nodded.

"He's back to his usual self," I answered honestly. "I, um...told him what happened. It's not like I could hide my eye."

She pressed her lips together as she looked me over, "No. Not really," she agreed. "How does it feel?"

"It was throbbing when I woke up, but I put an ice pack on it while making coffee and took some pain medicine."

"Good."

I could see the concern plainly all over her face, but I didn't really feel like talking about it. Lydia knew me, though, and simply reached over with her free hand to lace our fingers together. Just that simple touch had the lump shrinking, even if it was just a little. I brought our hands up to my lips and pressed a kiss to her knuckles.

Then we sipped on our drinks and enjoyed our rolls in silence, trying to make as little mess as possible in the bed. It was difficult not to let my thoughts wander back to last night, no matter how hard I tried to get past it. While that was the first time Grandad had ever laid hands on me, a part of me knew that this was just the beginning. Alzheimer's had a tendency to make people aggressive, no matter how kind of a soul they may be. Not that I could blame them. I'd be mad, too, if I was slowly forgetting myself.

Suddenly I felt Lydia give my hand a squeeze and I blinked a couple times as I returned to the present. It was often easy to get lost in the past or worrying about the future. But when I looked at Lydia, she just gave me a soft smile and another squeeze.

"Guess what?" she whispered, a sparkle in her eyes.

"What?"

"I love you."

Somehow she had said it even quieter than her prior whisper, but I heard it loud and clear. Those three words filled my body with warmth, chasing away the gloom of Grandad's disease and banishing it back to those dark corners it laid in wait for another time. There was nothing I could do except lean over and give her a solid kiss, letting it linger as if I could soak up her sunshine and positivity through her lips.

"I love you, too." I didn't even bother whispering, not caring at all who heard.

Chapter 23

Lydia

It was time for our weekly girls' dinner. Nicolette was hosting tonight at her flat and had decided it would be a themed dinner. Wanting to celebrate spring, she had opted for a floral theme even though it was still gray here in Scotland more often than not and somehow even rainier than usual. I opted for my floral print pajama set instead of a sundress, wanting to be comfortable when we inevitably piled onto the couch.

Nic had almost gone full Midsommar with a floral crown and maxi dress embroidered with flowers. Sofia, like usual, had gone much simpler with red rose earrings that matched the color of her nails.

"Those are so cute!" I complimented, leaning in for a better look. "And they look absolutely gorgeous with your dark hair."

Sofia always looked gorgeous, though. I'd never once seen her looking even the slightest bit frumpy.

She shyly tucked her hair behind her ear with a murmured, "Thank you."

"Viens, viens," Nic called, waving us over to her counter. Sofia and I just exchanged an amused look, but then joined her to see what she'd made. "I have lavender lemonade and if you are looking for some alcohol tonight like moi, I have made a batch with Lemoncello."

She then explained the snacks which included intricately arranged fruits, a charcuterie board with the meat slices rolled up like roses, and macarons with edible flowers pressed on top. It was more effort than we'd ever put into one of our girls' nights, but the fact was, we only had so many of these left.

With the oncoming of spring came the realization that there were only a few months left of the school year. You could sense it throughout the school; a certain buzz in the air as staff and students alike started counting down to the summer holiday. It, of course, held a different weight for us who were teaching abroad.

Deciding not to fret over it now, I filled up a plate and claimed a glass of the spiked lavender lemonade before finding a spot on the couch. I took a sip of the drink and my face instantly puckered.

"Damn, that's tart!" I laughed. "Whoo!"

Nic and Sofia were cackling, the latter of the two literally doubled over holding her stomach.

"Oh, I so wish I had a video of that. Your eye was literally twitching, Lyds," she gasped.

"I'm so glad you didn't."

I set the glass down for now, figuring I'd give it another shot when I truly needed a drink. Nic had gotten her food, but she hadn't sat yet, instead retrieving more goodies from her bedroom and laying them out on the coffee table.

"So, I also thought we could do that trend where you paint candles with melted wax," she explained before a rare, shy smile came over her face. "You know...as a little way to remember tonight and our girls' nights."

Sofia pouted up at her and her big, brown eyes somehow grew even bigger. "Oh, Nic!"

She tugged her down onto the couch between us so we could sandwich her into a hug. Nic was already sniffling, but then Sofia was joining her and even I had tears in my eyes.

"I love you girls so much. How on earth am I going to live without you?" Nic sobbed.

I soothingly ran my hand up and down her arm. "You aren't going to live without us. We'll have virtual girls' nights and catch each other up on our new crazy kids and coworkers," I promised.

Sofia sat up straighter, but kept her arm around Nic. "How are things going to work between you and Cass with you going back to France? Are you going to do long distance?"

She wiped away her tears, her fair brows pinched

together. "Quoi? Oh, no. I enjoyed being with Cass, but neither of us want long distance. We're okay with it. We had fun and that's what really matters."

My stomach twisted as I thought about Alec. Yes, I had consciously made the decision to pursue a relationship while on a work visa in a foreign country, but that didn't make it any easier thinking about going home.

I wasn't aware that my friends were now staring at me, both of them with the utmost sympathy.

"What about you and Alec? Have you talked about it?" Nic asked gently.

"No, I've been debating with myself still on what I want to do." I explained, settling back into my corner of the couch. My fingers fiddled with the hem of my pj shirt, running the soft fabric back and forth between the pads of my thumb and forefinger. "I think I may actually extend my contract."

Both of their jaws dropped, but I hurriedly explained before either of them could respond.

"And it's not because of Alec. I–" I took a deep breath, shaking my head. "I literally cannot fathom going back to the American education system. I've had stress dreams about it and wake up in a panic until I realize I'm still here. Scotland has been so good for me and I'm not ready to give that up."

Their shocked expressions quickly transformed into

ones of happiness and affection.

"I'm so proud of you."

"Yes! You stay away from that toxic ex of a country," Nic pumped her fist before looking at Sofia apologetically. "No offense."

Sofia just laughed and shook her head. "None taken. I'm going back simply because I miss my family like no other. And..." She grinned at us conspiratorially, "I found out that I'm going to be an aunt in a couple months."

Nic literally screamed and we were back into a giant hugging pile, this one now focusing on Sofia.

"That's so exciting!" I cried. "You are literally going to be the best auntie ever. That's one lucky baby."

Suddenly our drinks were being shoved into our hands and Nic held hers up for a toast. "To friendship, happiness, and love."

"Friendship, happiness, and love," we echoed before clinking our glasses together and taking a sip.

I managed not to pucker this time. At least not as much.

I held my throw pillow tight against my chest as I

listened to the infamous Skype ringtone, waiting on my parents to answer. I glanced once more at the time, double checking my math that this was a good time for them back home in Missouri. As if I didn't always Skype them around the same time.

Finally the ringing stopped and a few seconds later, my parents' smiling faces appeared on the screen, albeit a little pixelated. You'd think by now, the video quality would be better, but I suppose that's what I get for using Skype instead of Facetime. It was just easier to see both of them this way and this was definitely a conversation I wanted to be able to see them both properly and vice versa.

"Hello, darling!" My mother greeted me with a wide smile. "How are you?"

Clearly she hadn't registered the pillow in my clutches yet or she would have known something was up.

"I'm okay. How are you guys?"

They caught me up on their last few weeks, Dad complaining about his work messing up an order and him having to fix it like always and Mom raving about her dinner with some colleagues of hers at the new Italian restaurant in town. Hearing about such trivial things didn't help with me missing them and living close enough I could hear these stories on practically a daily basis.

"What about you, pumpkin? How are the kids doing with spring coming up?"

"Well, it's still super rainy, so not much has changed weather wise for them to notice," I joked lightly. "I do believe cabin fever is fully setting in, though. I may have them just put on their wellies and allow them to splash in puddles tomorrow."

My dad's eyebrows crinkled together and I couldn't help but laugh. "What on earth are 'wellies'?"

"Rain boots. That's what they call them here."

"You're clearly getting more comfortable with the slang, aren't you?" Mom noted.

My cheeks flushed and I ducked my head a little.

"Finally catching on after over half a year here. But...I'm sure I'll get better." This was a good enough transition as there would ever be, wasn't it? "I um...I'm going to renew my contract for another year here."

I chewed anxiously on my cheek as I waited for their response, not brave enough to look up and see the expressions on their faces even though I'd specifically wanted to Skype them for that very reason.

"That's wonderful!"

It took a moment for her response to sink in.

"Wait. Wonderful?" Now it was my turn to be confused.

My mom just laughed and nodded. "Yes. Wonderful."

"It's clear how much you love it there," Dad added. "You're practically glowing every time you talk about it. The kids, the city, the country."

"It's been such a blessing to see you thriving again. I've missed this version of you."

She looked as if she were tearing up and I knew I was about to full-on cry. Not because I was upset, but because I was utterly relieved. I sniffed hard to keep my nose from running and wiped at my eyes with the back of my hand.

"Me, too," I choked out, giving them a watery smile.

The last few years, I had either been at work or hidden away in my house under a fuzzy blanket, lacking any motivation or desire to do anything else. Now I was almost always doing something after work, whether it was being with Alec, playing Scrabble with Grandad, or spending time with my friends. I was rarely ever alone and I didn't need to be in order to cope with life. Being social recharged me now instead of draining me further. The last thing I wanted to do was waste time in my bedroom when I could be out exploring this beautiful country.

"We'll just have to plan another trip out there this summer while you are off and maybe we can go to some other countries," Dad shrugged before grinning. "Having a daughter in Europe is a pretty sweet deal if you ask me."

That at least made me laugh. "We can definitely visit other places."

"What did Alec say when you told him?" Mom asked curiously, a knowing smile on her face.

"I actually haven't told him yet. I wanted to make sure

it was official before I did."

"He'll be over the moon, I'm sure," Dad promised. "That man is head over heels for you. It was written all over his face."

That just made me blush even more that my dad had apparently noticed our feelings before we'd even shared them with each other. Had we been that obvious to everyone else?

"Well that's good because I've got it pretty bad for him, too."

Chapter 24

Lydia

I audibly gasped whenever we rounded the corner and just up the path, Midhope Castle stood at the top of the hill. Or for any *Outlander* fan, Lallybroch. It was quite crazy seeing it in person. It felt like I'd stepped into the show, back in time to the 1700s. Minus the people in modern clothing milling about the grounds, of course.

Alec gave a soft chuckle beside me and gently tugged me further along the path. I'd gone on several day trips with the girls to different places, but I knew Alec would appreciate this location since he'd actually read the books and seen the show. Even if he wasn't as into it as I was.

"Do ye want me to take a picture of ye?" he offered, loosening his grip on my hand and slowing his step.

"Only if you take one with me, too."

"I can do that."

I walked further up the path and then turned, smiling widely as Alec held up his phone, stepping to the right a little as he lined up the shot.

"I tried to position ye so ye blocked the other tourists.

Hopefully it turned out alright."

He strode towards me and held out his phone for my inspection. The castle looked nothing but stunning behind me and he had managed to make it seem as if I were the only one here.

"I love it! Now one with my own Jamie," I winked up at him with a grin.

He playfully rolled his eyes before looking around and spotting a man roughly our age coming up the path. I waited as he walked down to him, clearly asking if the man would mind taking our picture. Then Alec was jogging back to my side and slipping his arm around my waist. Instinctively I wrapped my arm around him in return and tucked myself into his side, smiling once more.

"Just a second," the kind stranger called out. "Just waiting on this fella to move. Okay...now smile!"

He was quick and efficient, bringing us Alec's phone to check the photo before he continued up to the castle.

"Thank you so much. We really appreciate it," I gushed.

"No problem," he smiled politely and then was on his way.

Alec tucked his phone back into his pocket and then nodded towards the castle. "Shall we follow?"

I just nodded and took his hand in mine once more.

"Ye called me your own Jamie, but if I recall correctly, I look a bit more like his dad. He had dark hair, no? And his mam red hair like him?"

I pursed my lips as I tried to recall the details. They hadn't exactly shown his parents very often in the tv series. Or at least only his father in a few scenes.

"I believe so. But I am also totally okay with being Ellen and Brian Fraser. They had quite the romantic love story."

A certain smile came to Alec's face. Not his typical full smile and not the quiet one he used when I amused him in some way, but he didn't want to let me know. No, this smile was more reminiscent and I'd seen it a handful of times.

"I know of another romantic love story about an Ellen. Although she married a Fergus."

Of course. His grandmother was named Ellen. That's why it rang a bell and more importantly the reasoning behind his conflicted smile. Even though she had passed four years ago, the loss still greatly affected Alec. Possibly even more so because of living with his Grandad. It wasn't unusual for him to forget the passing of his beloved wife and search for her. It'd happened a few times when I had been visiting Grandad alone and it absolutely tore my heart out. I couldn't imagine how those moments felt for Alec.

I soothingly rubbed my thumb along his, leaning into his arm more.

"I'm sure it's an even more romantic story than the ones in movies and novels."

The corner of his lips twitched once more and he finally looked down at me, that far away look fading from his eyes as he came back to the now.

"Grandad and I started writing it down," he shared before laughing and shaking his head. "I'll just say, it was not exactly love at first sight. Or maybe it was and they just didn't know what to do with that."

"Well I can't wait to read it," I grinned.

Since the castle had been neglected and wasn't open for the public to go inside, we mostly walked around the outside and took pictures before heading back to the car to find more places on the estate to explore.

Hopetoun Estate was absolutely stunning. It was perfect timing to visit in the spring, the appropriately named Spring Garden in full bloom.

That was where we decided to have our picnic lunch. While it wasn't as extravagant of a meal as we'd had on our first picnic date, we still had a fairly good set up and a beautiful view. Scotland's scenery never ceased to take my breath away.

After months of gray skies and rain or snow, I was more than happy to soak up the sunlight, stretched out on the picnic blanket with my head resting on Alec's lap. His fingers idly ran through the ends of my hair, slowly working out the tangles. Between that and my full stomach, I could easily fall asleep. My eyes were already closed.

But of course, I was thinking about the news I had to share with Alec. Just the idea of it gave me butterflies in my stomach and made my heart race even though I knew he'd be happy. Or at least I hoped he would be.

"Alec?" I opened my eyes to look up at him.

"Hmm?"

He had been zoned out, his gaze on my hair as he played with it, but now his eyes met mine. For a moment, I couldn't swallow, my mouth dry. I slowly sat up and turned on the blanket to face him. Best to just say it.

"I renewed my contract with the school."

His eyebrows crinkled in confusion and I could practically see the gears turning in his head as he tried to process what I was saying.

"Wait–" He closed his eyes and shook his head as if to clear any leftover haze before looking at me more intently. "You're..."

"Staying," I finished for him. "I'm staying here in Scotland."

"I didn't even know that was an option."

Finally realization began to dawn and his entire face lit up. Before I knew it, he was cupping my face and pulling me in for a big kiss. I couldn't help but giggle against his lips at his reaction. Also because I was just so damn happy. I knew this was the right decision. I felt it in my bones each time I told someone.

He pulled back, but his hands stayed where they were, thumbs brushing absently across my cheeks. His warm brown eyes just scanned my face and I felt myself flush under his gaze.

"Staying was really my only option. There's nothing for me in Missouri besides my parents. I'd have to find a new place to live and there's absolutely no way that I could go back to teaching there. I'd have to find another job." I took his hands from my cheeks and held them in my lap, fiddling with his fingers. "I love the kids here, I love my school, and that's something I never thought I'd say again. I've just fallen in love with Scotland in general."

"Aye, and did I have nothing to do with your decision?" he teased. "Ye know. Just the Scot that ye fell in love with."

I laughed and gave his hands a squeeze. "Believe me. You were a big factor." I leaned in for a quick kiss. "You mean so much to me, Alec. I'm not ready to let you go."

"Good," he mumbled, stealing another. "I haven't been ready to let ye go since I ran into ye outside the bookshop."

"You learned your lesson after letting go of me at the show," I teased.

Now it was his turn to let out a hearty laugh, head falling back, but then he was nodding. "Aye. I did. I'll never make that mistake again."

I don't know how long we sat there, just holding hands

and smiling at each other like lovesick teens. Alec turned my hands over in his and interlaced our fingers, bringing them both up to rest against his lips. Again, I could see the gears turning.

"Ye ken Grandad will get worse, aye?"

I bit the inside of my lip, but nodded. "Yes."

The disease had progressed more as of late and it was becoming more apparent how much Grandad needed Orla and Alec around to care for him.

"I want to be here with you. With both of you. To support you however I can."

He closed his eyes and pressed his lips hard to my knuckles. I just held onto him tighter.

"You Morgan men have stolen my heart and there's nothing anyone can do about it," I tried to lighten the mood.

It was true, though. I'd take whatever time I could with both of them and cherish every second. That made him grin at least. I could feel his lips curling against my knuckles.

"I must say, the feeling is mutual. Ye easily charmed the both of us from the start."

Alec

"How was it?" Grandad greeted us when we returned home, pausing his episode of *Fawlty Towers*.

"Absolutely stunning!" Lydia gushed.

I set the picnic basket down, making a mental note to put it away later. "She audibly gasped when she saw Midhope Castle."

Lydia lightly tapped my arm with the back of her hand which just made me laugh. Then she took the open seat next to Grandad and began to tell him about our day, showing him the pictures we'd taken even if he'd seen the estate before.

Orla walked in from the dining room, carrying a tray of fresh tea. She was always predicting exactly what you would need without you saying it.

"Thank you, Orla."

"Well ye didna let me make anything for the picnic, so I wanted to be useful somehow," she waved her hand dismissively.

I scoffed playfully, "I canna have ye making all of our date meals. You'll spoil Lydia and then nothing I prepare will ever compare to your cooking."

"Sounds like I'll just have to teach ye, then. Though I

dinna think we have much time left."

I could see the wistful look in her eyes as she looked at Lydia and Grandad. We weren't the only ones that had grown used to her presence. Orla had a soft spot for her as well. I don't believe there was a single person I knew that didn't like Lydia. How could they not?

"Actually...we may have more time than you think."

Orla just gave me a curious look, but then I was turning to Lydia and giving her a little nudge. I didn't even have to tell her; just with a look she knew exactly what I was thinking.

"I have an announcement." She paused and glanced around the room at each of us. "I have decided to extend my contract and will be teaching here in Scotland for at least another year."

My heart did a little flip in my chest at the addition of 'at least'. I could only hope for more and more time with her.

Orla let out a squeal, her hands fluttering up to cover her mouth. "Oh, how wonderful!" she gushed.

Grandad just let out a hearty laugh and pulled her into a hug. Somehow I felt even more elated than I had when she had told me at our picnic. Seeing her hugging Grandad just as tightly hit me differently. There'd been no falter in her voice or any hint of insecurity when she told me she was more than willing to stay and support the both of us through the inevitable changes the future brought.

I had no choice, but to witness it all. Even though it had been my choice to be the one to come and care for him, to say 'no' had never even crossed my mind. Of course, I would be there for him. But Lydia had a choice. She was not related to him, she'd only known him for less than a year. She could easily leave and forever think of him as how he was in this current moment without having to witness the decay. That didn't matter to my Lydia, though.

The future was terrifying for me to think about. The loss was inevitable, as well as the pain and frustration that came with it. It seemed just the slightest bit more bearable knowing that I would have her by my side. Sure, her presence wouldn't fix Grandad and wouldn't stop the disease from progressing, but at least I wouldn't be alone in it. There would be my person that I could turn to and vent to without fear of sounding ridiculous or pitiful. She would love me through it all without my asking.

Once Grandad let go of her, Lydia was instantly reaching for my hand and holding it between both of hers in her lap. Even though Orla was still gushing about how happy she was, my eyes were locked on Lydia's. The highland hill green of her irises and the absolute warmth that shined out of them. My sunshine. Mine.

Chapter 25

Lydia

While I was not as great of a party planner as Nicolette was, I had tried my best to plan a going away party for Nic and Sofia. Grandad had been so kind as to let us have the dinner party in his garden which was blooming beautifully. The weather had also been kind enough to cooperate with us and the sun shined down warmly.

Alec was finishing setting the table just as I brought out the candle holders with the floral candles I had painted at Nic's, figuring she would like the sentimental touch. She'd honestly probably end up crying, but then again, I had a feeling there would be a lot of tears tonight no matter what.

Sofia's flight left tomorrow morning and Alec and I had promised to take her. Nic was planning on staying with Cass tonight for one last rendezvous before she flew back to Paris. They had been so adorable together, it was bittersweet to think of it ending, but it just made me even more grateful that I wasn't having to say goodbye to my love.

Speak of the devil, he was suddenly by my side, gently

resting his hand on the small of my back.

"Where'd ye go there, hen?" he asked with a light chuckle. "Ye zoned out on me."

My cheeks flushed slightly as I let go of my grip on the chair and instead turned to him.

"Just thinking. Lots to think about really."

He bent down to press his lips to my forehead. "Don't think too hard, aye? Ye've got plenty of time for all the emotions once the girls get here."

"Actually," I reached up to fiddle with the fabric of his t-shirt, picking off invisible lint. "I was thinking about how lucky I am that I don't have to say goodbye to you."

I peeked shyly up at him to find him smiling, which just made me smile in return. Now both of his arms were wrapped around my waist and he was pulling me securely into his chest. I happily nuzzled into him, holding him tight.

"I'd say I'm the lucky one. Get to keep my hen. My sunshine."

I was glad he couldn't see my face since it was securely hidden against his chest, so my burning cheeks were a secret.

"And I get to keep my safe place. My haven."

He was quiet for a moment or two before he spoke up again. "Is that me? Or Scotland?"

I just laughed, shaking my head, and then pulled back

to look at him. "You, silly." I gave his sides a squeeze.

"Well that's what I was hoping for."

Suddenly the back door flung open and the unmistakable voice of Nicolette rang out across the garden.

"Alright, my little lovebirds, enough cuddling! You've got plenty of time for all that, but I only get to be with my besties for another night."

I playfully rolled my eyes as Alec and I dropped our arms from around each other and turned to face her and Sofia. Even though Nic was smiling mischievously, I could still see the sparkle of emotion in her eyes before she was hugging me. We squeezed each other tight, pulling Sofia into the mix.

"It's not our last night. We'll be together again," Sofia promised. "We'll just have to plan a trip to visit you in France."

"Yes!" Nic gasped, pulling back with renewed excitement. "Come and eat all the delicious desserts."

That was all she had to say, knowing that neither myself or Sofia could turn down desserts. Especially not decadent French desserts.

"So is this a girls only trip or...?" Alec teased.

Nic just eyed him which made me giggle. Bless Alec for having put up with the three of us for so long.

We finally sat down at the table, after Sofia had snapped several pictures of the set up, and began to fill up our plates from the variety of dishes laid out. Orla had been an absolute saint helping me cook while the men hid out in the library, making the smart decision to stay out of our way. Orla really had no patience for anyone interfering when she was cooking.

Before anyone began to eat, I took my wine glass and carefully pushed my chair back to stand up.

"I'd like to start us off with a toast of sorts." I took a deep breath as I looked around the table. "I had no idea what to expect when I boarded that plane in Missouri and I know there is no way on earth I could have predicted what lay ahead.

"I met two wonderful friends who inspire me, both as a teacher and as a woman. Nic," I looked across the table to her. "You have such a love for life and I was happy to tag along on all of your adventures. You taught me how to make teaching fun again and I'm forever grateful for the joy you've helped me bring into the classroom."

Now she really was teary-eyed, but for once she was speechless. I took advantage of the rare silence from her and directed my attention to Sofia.

"Sofia. You were my beacon this past year, keeping me tethered to home and helping me focus on what's really important. You are the most gentle and loving teacher."

I retrieved two small boxes from under my seat and handed each of them one. Inside was a silver necklace with a trinity knot pendant. Sofia softly gasped whenever she opened the lid and Nicolette had the necklace out of the box in seconds.

"Grandad explained to me that in Celtic culture, the number three is very significant. So I thought that this trinity knot was a perfect reminder for all of us of our friendship. Even though we won't be just down the hall from each other anymore, I know that the distance will not come in between us. You both are forever my sisters."

Now came the waterworks. Nic had dropped her necklace to the table in favor of shoving her chair back and rushing around to hug me. Sofia was right behind her, at a more reasonable pace, of course, and we were all crying as we hugged each other. Then we just laughed at ourselves for being so emotional.

"What about Alec?" Nic suddenly cried out.

All of our heads lifted and turned to Alec who was still sitting in his seat next to me.

"Can I make a toast to Alec since you're staying here with him?"

I opened and closed my mouth like a fish, looking to Alec for his opinion, but he just laughed and shrugged. Nic and Sofia returned to their seats, but stayed standing as they lifted their glasses again. I took that as my cue to sit down.

"Alec, thank you for loving our Lydia. The relationship

you two have is absolutely beautiful and I'm so glad you found each other," Sofia started with a soft smile.

"Even after you ditched her the first time you met," Nic added.

I covered my face, laughing and shaking my head while Sofia gave her a nudge in the side with her elbow.

"Seriously, though, I know you will look after our girl and love her like she deserves. And that is all we can ask for."

The sentiment was sweet and it meant a lot to me that my friends thought just as highly of Alec as I did. Before I could say anything or finally take a sip of my drink, Nic began to tap her spoon against her glass over and over.

"Now, kiss, kiss!"

My cheeks were full on burning now, but then Alec was cupping my chin between his fingers and turning my head to give me a sweet kiss, letting it linger solely for my friends' benefit since neither of us were big on excessive PDA.

"Okay, so does this mean I get to do a toast for Lydia?" he asked once he was settled back in his chair.

"Oh, no, no. You don't have to," I insisted.

He stood anyway as Nic and Sofia eagerly sat back down, looking up at him expectantly. I, myself, was nervously biting on my bottom lip. Getting to praise my friends and thank them was one thing, but having the attention on me was another.

"Hen," he started before shaking his head and glancing around the table. "Sorry. Lydia. I am so proud of you. While none of us knew ye the previous few years, we know how difficult they were for ye and we are so lucky to have been able to witness ye bloom and thrive this past year. You have brought so much light and love to those of us here, to my family, and I know to your school. We are all grateful that we get to be a part of this journey for you."

Yup. I was crying before he even got halfway through. Alec was merely a blur as the tears ran down my cheeks and I quickly reached for my cloth napkin to wipe them away.

Life had been hard on me for a long time and Scotland had been my attempt at escape. It ended up being so much more than an escape, though. It was a fresh start, a new beginning, the first chapter of a much happier story. I cherished all of the new characters deeply and appreciated every bit of the plot, both the highs and lows. I felt like myself again, but at the same time as though I was a completely different person. Either way, I really liked this Lydia. I had fallen for the Scot, I had fallen for Scotland, but ultimately I had fallen in love with life again and that was more than I could ever ask for.

Epilogue

Alec

"Smile!" Mrs. Foster called.

We'd been smiling for the last several seconds as she tried to figure out how to take the picture. My cheeks were going to be sore after this.

"Okay, now toss!"

I made my wish and tossed the coin over my shoulder, hearing the soft plunk as it hit the water and then slowly floated to the bottom. I looked to Lydia, who still had her coin firmly clasped in her fist. Yet her face was serene, eyes closed as she apparently thought over her wish. Leave it to Lydia to overthink something like a wish at the Trevi Fountain. Finally, she tossed the coin over her shoulder and turned to watch it sink.

"What did ye wish for?" I asked.

Lydia's jaw dropped in disbelief. "Do you not want my wish to come true?"

I just laughed and shook my head before holding my hands up defensively.

"Okay. My bad. I was just curious since it seemed to

take ye so long to decide."

She clearly wanted to roll her eyes at me, but managed to resist. I knew that look of hers well, though.

"It was hard coming up with something when I've got so many things to be thankful for already," she replied matter-of-factly. "I'm in Rome with my parents and my wonderful boyfriend; I get to spend another year in Scotland; and I love my job again. I'm happy."

I didn't even care if her parents were just standing a few feet away and we were surrounded by hundreds of strangers speaking in all different languages. I cupped her cheeks in both of my hands and kissed her. She seemed shocked at first, but quickly responded, wrapping her small hands around my wrists as she returned the kiss.

"I love you, hen," I murmured.

She smiled, "I love you, too. And I love our story."

"It's nowhere near being over yet."

Not if the Trevi Fountain granted my wish.

Acknowledgements

First of all, I want to thank the creators of Celtic music playlists on YouTube. Thank you for being the soundtrack to my writing and helping me get into the mindset of Scotland, even in the midst of a Missouri winter and spring.

Thank you to my writing buddy, Lori, for going on this journey with me and loving Alec and Lydia as much as I do. Thank you for your insight and advice over the years. It has been wonderful seeing each of us grow as authors.

Shout out to Gabby for being the trailblazer and showing me that publishing my own book is possible. I couldn't have done it without your reassurance and leadership.

Thank you, Mom, for being my secondary editor. It was so encouraging to have an avid reader like you enjoy my story so much. Thank you, Dad, for giving me your wanderlust and love of Celtic heritage. Thank you to the both of you for always supporting me in whatever venture I decide to go on next!

Want more Alec and Lydia?

With time ticking away on her work visa, both Lydia and Alec are concerned not just about her job, but also the future of their relationship. She hopes a tarot reading from her visiting internet friend, Sabrina, will provide guidance. But what if it suggests a solution that she never allowed herself to consider?

Ringing in the New Year: A Hogmanay Holiday Novella is a collaborative epilogue combining the characters from *Falling for Scotland* and *The Fate Date* by Clover Callahan.

About the Author

Kaitlin Collins is an elementary teacher and avid traveler based in the Kansas City, Missouri area. She lives with a menagerie of pets, including her bunny (Artemis), leopard gecko (Bruni), and puppy (Ringo). Books and writing have been her escape for years and she is excited to share these characters and their story with the world.

Instagram, Threads, and TikTok: @booksbykaitlin